Winter

For the Best in Literature

Winter

JOHN MARSDEN

SCHOLASTIC INC.

New York Toronto London Auckland Sydney
Mexico City New Delhi Hong Kong Buenos Aires

ISBN 0-439-36850-2

Copyright © 2000 by Graywood Crest Pty Ltd.
All rights reserved. Published by Scholastic Inc.
Scholastic, POINT, and associated logos are trademarks and/or registered trademarks of Scholastic Inc.

First published in Macmillan by Pan Macmillan Australia Pty Limited

Scholastic hardcover edition, August 2002

12 11 10 9 8 7 6 5 4 3 2 1   4 5 6 7 8/0

Printed in the U.S.A.   01

First paperback printing, January 2004

To Callie Stephen,
wishing you many happy endings

Winter

CHAPTER ONE

I CAME HOME WHEN I WAS SIXTEEN.
Ralph picked me up at the station.

It was a high step into the Range Rover. It looked like Ralph had cleaned out the front by chucking all his stuff over the seat. It was a mess back there, a jumble of jackets and tools and wire, a chain saw and an oil drum.

At first I thought Ralph was the same as he'd been in Canberra, but as we passed the 80k sign on our way out of Christie, I started to realize he was nervous.

Nervous of me, I mean.

For one thing he was talking too much. The more people talk at me, the more silent I get. Maybe that's one reason I make some people nervous. They don't know what I'm thinking when I go quiet.

What would the Robinsons have told Ralph about me? I could guess some of it. "Willful. Headstrong. Won't take no for an answer. Wants her own way all the time."

Knowing them, they'd probably have gone further. "Never thinks of others. Spoiled and selfish. I know it's not a nice thing to say, but . . ."

I sighed and leaned back, closing my eyes. How come you can't escape people's voices, even when you've left them for good? I thought I'd got rid of the Robinsons, but there they were again, in my ears. The trouble was, this time they were coming at me from the inside instead of the outside. It was worse.

We left the flat country, the paddocks of nothing, the barbed-wire fences running like stitches on bare skin. Gradually we started winding up into the hills. The turn-off to Warriewood was on a sharp bend. We swung right, onto the dirt, and drove down less than a kilometer to the front gate.

I so wanted this moment to be profound. I wanted to stand at the gate and drink it all in, gazing at the stone pillars and the spaces for the coach lamps, at the long drive lined with rhododendrons and hydrangeas. I wanted to see what had been just wisps in my mind, and bring the vague dreams and memories back to life.

Ralph didn't hesitate though; he turned into the driveway with one easy swing of the steering wheel. We passed the homestead and the barn and the little yellow cottage where Grandma used to live, and went on up to the manager's house. It all happened so quickly that we were there before I had time to notice anything.

Sylvia came out of the house, wiping her hands on a tea towel. "Well, well, well," she said. "Here you are, back again. After all this time. I wouldn't have known you. I would have walked past you in the street."

Sylvia was trying to be cozy and friendly but luke-warm was the best she could do. Ralph was softer than Sylvia.

"Come in," she said. "I've put the kettle on. But I don't know, are you a tea or coffee drinker? Or would you rather have cordial? I have to keep cordial in the house for Ralph. He's got such a sweet tooth."

At their front door I stopped. I suddenly felt that if I went in there I'd never come out again. Not literally of course. I mean, they weren't going to murder me. But if I started off going straight into their house, their territory, I'd be trapped. I felt I had to start strongly, more strongly than this.

I didn't feel strong. The train trip had taken nine hours, with the change at Exley, and I hadn't slept for more than a couple of minutes. But I called up all the energy I could find. I felt my fists clench.

"No thanks. I want to go and look at the homestead first."

"Oh you don't want to do that. Not after such a long journey. There'll be time to explore later."

She was already turning to go inside the house, assuming I was following. From behind me Ralph added: "A cup of tea's what you want."

I felt the pressure. It was like a tractor pushing from behind, and a tow truck pulling from in front.

3

"No," I said. I spat it out. Not only my fists were clenched now, but my teeth as well. "No. I'm going to look at the homestead."

They both stopped, like I'd sworn at them. Sylvia couldn't meet my eyes. I'd acted in such a bad-mannered bad-tempered way that they were embarrassed for me. My face was hot.

"Well," Sylvia said. "Of course, if that's what you want."

She looked over my head at Ralph and a message seemed to flicker between them.

"I'll go with you," Ralph said from behind.

"No," I said. "I want to go on my own."

I knew the strength had ebbed out of my voice. My words sounded weak, even to me.

"I'll have to come," Ralph said. "The keys are hidden by the woodshed. You'll need me to show you where they are."

He'd won the first set, but at least I'd got it to a tiebreaker. In spite of that I felt like a little child as I followed him meekly down the hill. It was nearly six o'clock, and not much daylight left. We crossed a stone bridge over a small dam. Above me was a wisteria, just bare brown branches now. To my right a blackberry snaked along the bridge, looking for another patch of soft accommodating soil where it could put down roots. To the left the water was black with mud or decayed leaves, I wasn't sure which. A single white Muscovy duck sat on a log, looking at me with friendly interest. I hoped it was friendly anyway. I felt like nothing here could be taken on trust.

We turned right and walked down the slope, under the avenue of elms to the homestead. Although no one had painted it in a long time, the white was strong enough to stand out. Apart from the white walls and green roof, it was just like the photograph, the one that had sat on my dressing table all these years.

But with Ralph right beside me I couldn't feel anything. No, that's not true, I felt a lot. But I couldn't show a hint of it to him, and because I couldn't trust myself to hide it I couldn't let myself feel it. I set my mouth in a hard line and waited as he scrabbled among the firewood before pulling out a bunch of old keys.

"Here we go," he said.

Because Ralph had been so friendly at the station, I didn't say what I wanted to: "Get out. I have to do this on my own." The best I could manage was: "I'll be OK on my own," but he ignored that. I'm not sure if he heard it even.

I felt a little sick as we approached the house. The main door into the homestead is kind of the back door, because it gives the easiest access to the woodboxes and the laundry, the sheds and the paddocks. The official front door opens onto a nice wide veranda but it's a steep walk up the hill to get to it. There's a white gravel path and a set of steps if you're coming that way.

We stepped onto the back veranda. There were pools of water all the way along and I nearly put my foot through a rotting floorboard. Ralph was sorting through the keys and didn't seem to notice.

"How long since anyone lived here?" I asked him.

He gave me a startled glance. "No one since you," he said.

He seemed so surprised I didn't know that. I was angry I didn't know it, didn't know nearly enough. That's the trouble with stuff that happens when you're little. People assume you know it but most of the time you don't.

I was glad no one had lived here though. I didn't want it desecrated. Better to have it fall down than that.

And falling down seemed like quite a possibility. As Ralph fumbled to find a key that would fit the lock, I had time to look around. It was no wonder there were pools of water along the veranda, because half the weatherboards above me were sagging, and strands of ivy were growing through a few. The paint on the wall had blistered and peeled away. I felt cold. I pushed my hands up my jumper and hunched my shoulders, trying to stop whatever warmth was in me from leaving my body.

Ralph got the door open and went in.

I guess I was in the mood to be aggravated, and nothing that day aggravated me as much as Ralph going in ahead of me. My house, my home, and Ralph went first.

Maybe it was good in one way, because it gave me the courage and determination to do what I wanted to do.

I followed him in, still hugging myself.

It didn't smell too bad, that was one good thing. It was musty but I'd been preparing myself for worse, so I didn't mind it much. The carpet looked OK, and the place seemed dry.

Ralph was standing in the middle of the first room, looking at me to see how I'd react. I made my face even stonier, and ignored him. The room was narrow but ran the width of the house. It had no furniture.

"This was the sunroom," Ralph said. "Your father added this back section. They used it as a breakfast room, I think."

I nodded. I had only a vague memory of it.

I walked past Ralph and on into the next room. This was the kitchen, and as soon as I came through the door I got a rush of images so fast that they spilled over each other. It was like a train wreck in my mind. I stood there, confused. I wanted to grab at each memory so as not to lose it, but I was worried that as I grabbed at one the next would rush past and be gone.

I felt like the monkey with his paw in the jar, so greedy to seize a handful of peanuts that he can't get his arm out, and is caught by the hunters who've left the jar as a trap. In my handful of memories was the whooshing noise of a fire in the chimney, and a smell of popcorn, and my mother — or someone — making me fairy bread with a face of chocolate bits. I remembered getting in trouble for trying to eat a firelighter, and burning myself when I tipped over a coffee mug, and watching a mouse writhing in a trap and feeling distressed to see it.

Flavors, smells, colors, cold food and hot food, meals and snacks and drinks . . . my mind wasn't so much like a handful of memories as a smorgasbord. I hardly noticed that the kitchen, like the sunroom, was bare and empty. There was a fuel stove, and a gas range, but nothing else.

I walked from room to room, Ralph tagging behind. The sitting room and dining room jogged nothing in my memory, but when we got to the bedrooms something started to happen. In the main one I had a vivid image of a big old bed — oak, I think — and a lot of big, heavy furniture that all matched. And a soft, soft eiderdown with a cover of purple flowers.

I turned to Ralph. "What's happened to the furniture?"

He looked uncomfortable. "Oh, well . . . you know

how it is, it gradually went, piece by piece. Borer, for instance. Then, water got through the roof in a few places, wrecked some bits."

I didn't say anything, just went on into the small bedroom in the right-hand corner of the homestead. I knew where I was now. The light-blue walls still had the feeling of a spring sky, even if they were faded and worn. My bed had been in the middle, with a view of the palm tree out the front window and the hedge with little red flowers to the right. There'd been a chest of drawers in the corner between the two windows, and against the wall a wardrobe that backed onto the corridor. My teddies and dolls and soft toys had lived on top of the chest of drawers — the dolls that didn't fit into the bed, anyway.

I glanced at the wall behind me, the corner beside the door. My heart gave a little jump, like it had sneezed. In a plain old gold frame was a picture of a dark hill and crescent moon, viewed as if through an open window. Under the picture was a poem that I knew by heart.

Sweet be thy sleep, my guest,
Peace come to thee, and rest,
Throughout all the quiet night,
And with the morning light,
Awake thee and rise refreshed.

Funny, as the words echoed through my mind it was not my own voice I was hearing. Someone was reading the words to me. Who? I wondered. It was a woman's voice, soft and calm. My mother's? That I didn't know. And I would never know.

We went through the front door and stood on the veranda. Away to the west the sun was dropping like a rock. A fiery volcanic rock.

Ralph cleared his throat. "Well, time we were getting back," he said in a low voice.

Suddenly I knew I could never sleep in their house, the way they'd arranged. Astonished at the words I heard coming from my mouth, I said: "I'm going to sleep here tonight."

CHAPTER TWO

TEA WITH RALPH AND SYLVIA was sulky and unpleasant. I felt sorry for Sylvia in one way, because she'd gone to a lot of trouble to make a special meal. Pumpkin and chilli soup, lamb cutlets on rice, with a potato and turnip mixture in a baking dish. The potato and turnip didn't really seem to go with the lamb and rice, but what would I know? I'm no food expert.

I got through most of my soup because, face it, no matter how bad you feel you can usually pour soup down your throat. Plus I quite like stuff with chilli. I ate the rice and about two mouthfuls of lamb. I mean, I'm not a full-on vegetarian, but I don't eat much meat, and only then if I'm in the mood. I hate turnips.

I might have got away with just that little amount, but Sylvia produced a raspberry cheesecake, and I knew my stomach would revolt if I tried to shove that down. So I said no, as politely as I could, and Sylvia pushed back her chair, threw down her spoon, and stormed into the kitchen.

I sat there feeling awful. My face was as hot as a fuel stove, and I knew my bottom lip had the shakes, and if I tried to say anything the tears quivering in my eyes would break free and run down my cheeks.

I couldn't take any more. The argument when I said I wanted to sleep in the homestead had taken too much out of me.

When you're a teenager, if you want something badly enough and you're prepared to go to any lengths to get it, you can pretty much always win. I'd learned that with the Robinsons, and I'd learned it at school. The tantrums I'd chucked with the Robinsons were full-on. Like, Hell's Angels meets the Gay and Lesbian Mardi Gras. Like, a Rugby League Grand Final. I was embarrassed when I thought about them. Ashamed even. But in the end I got what I wanted. I was back here. Back home. On my own. And I was out of school.

I'd thought that once I got here it would all be perfect. My problems would be over.

No such luck. There I was, acting like I was still at the Robinsons'. Within two hours of getting off the train I'd gone straight back into tantrum territory.

Maybe there was a better way of getting what I wanted. But if there was, I didn't know about it. No one had taught me. It was one of those times I felt bitter about not having parents. I felt like I'd grown up without guide posts, without a street directory. How did other people solve their problems, convince others to let them do stuff? The Robinsons didn't really count. They were so old and they hardly talked to each other, let alone to me. They seemed like they had everything they wanted anyway — for the way they lived. Wasn't much fun for a kid. But they had their antique furniture and their car and their afternoon teas and the tennis club, and Mrs. Robinson loved shopping. They didn't need ways to solve problems, because for them a big problem was missing garbage night, or having a stain on the upholstery of the Audi.

When I started my campaign to leave school and come back to Warriewood, they were like, "What is happening here? Who is this alien invading our house?"

The scene with Sylvia had been like the Robinsons revisited.

"I want to sleep in the homestead."

"You can't do that. There's no furniture."

"I don't care."

"Look, Winter, it's not possible. There's no bed even."

"I'll sleep on the floor."

"Well, that's just ridiculous."

"I don't give a shit if it's ridiculous or not."

"We've got a nice room for you here. The bed's all made up, and dinner's nearly ready."

"I told you, I'm not sleeping here. I'm sleeping in the homestead."

"You can't sleep there on your own. Just stay with

us for a few days and we'll see if we can sort something out."

At that point I picked up my bag and started for the door.

"Winter, where are you going?"

"Where do you think?"

"No, look, wait a minute. This is just crazy. Honestly, Winter, this is not the way to do things. In the morning I'll see if Ralph can move a bed in and then perhaps you can camp there for a night, if that's what you want."

"I'm staying there tonight and every night. I'm back for good."

I opened the door and went out into the cool evening air. It was dark outside. Really dark. I could hear Sylvia's voice. "Ralph, do something. Stop her."

I snapped. I stood there in the blackness. I screamed back at them. The one thing I'd promised myself I wouldn't say. The one thing that was unforgivable.

"This is my property and I'll do what I want."

There was a silence inside. I wondered if I'd made both of them disappear. In that blackness anything was possible.

Then Ralph came out. He went to take my bag but I wouldn't let him. I backed off, half a dozen steps.

"I was just going to carry it there for you," he said mildly.

"I can carry it myself," I said.

"Well, I'll get the truck and bring a bed down."

"I'll give you a hand."

It was quite a business. We had to fetch the truck from a garage then unlock the barn and go up into the loft and drag out a mattress and four different sections of a bed. We got it into the homestead, into my old bedroom, then Ralph realized he'd forgotten a screwdriver, so it was back to the barn to get that.

When he said, "Now how about coming back to the house for a spot of dinner?" I had another of my attacks of weakness and shame, and said, "Yeah, OK, thanks."

But it hadn't been such a good idea, judging by the effect I'd had on Sylvia.

I left their house, ignoring Ralph as he followed me out the door saying, "You don't have to go to the homestead now. You can stay here and watch TV. Don't worry about Sylvia, she's just a bit stressed."

It wasn't as dark as before, because the moon had come up over the hill, behind the orchard. It was dark enough though, and I stumbled a few times as I headed towards the duck dam. At one point I thought I'd lost my way, which had me panicking, but then I saw the silhouette of the homestead, like a lighthouse, and from then on I was OK.

We hadn't locked it again after delivering the bed. There was a light on the veranda somewhere but I didn't know where to find the switch, so I didn't waste time looking. Instead I opened the door and groped my way into the sunroom.

It was just so dark. The air felt stale. The faintest wisp of cobweb drifted across my face and caught on my eyebrows. For a few moments, as I spread my hands across the wall trying to find the switch, I felt sick. I didn't know what I was doing there. I didn't know what would become of me. I didn't know where to find the bloody switch.

It was such a relief to feel it under my fingers. Things got a bit easier after that. Using the light from the sunroom I turned the kitchen lights on, and worked my way through the house flicking every switch I could find. Only then did I feel a bit safer.

Ralph and I had already set up the bed in my bedroom, using Ralph's trusty screwdriver. But I've never seen anything so lonely as that little bed sitting in the bare cold room. I brought in my bag and started unpacking. That helped a little, to see my familiar belongings. The worst thing was that there was no bedding. I'd planned to get some from Sylvia, but with all the tension at teatime I hadn't got around to it, and no way in the world was I going back for it now.

I didn't even have a pillow, but I rolled up my PJs and used them. Then I went through the house turning the lights out again. Back in my bedroom I got a parka and my tracky-daks, and put those on over my clothes, then stretched out on the mattress.

It wasn't very comfortable. I got the feeling I'd be pretty cold by morning. I'd brought a book with me, *The Butcher Boy*, and I'd read half of it on the train, but I couldn't be bothered reading any more now. And I had my Discman, but I'd flattened the batteries on the train playing Lena Horne over and over.

I didn't really want to play any more CDs though. I wanted to feel . . . something. Whatever was waiting for me in the homestead, whatever was waiting to be felt. I wanted to experience that. I got up again and turned off the last light, and groped my way back to bed.

It was kind of early but I didn't care. There was nothing else to do. And I was pretty tired from the train journey.

Most of all though, I was hoping something powerful would happen, in the dark of my own room, back in my own home for the first time in twelve years.

I lay there trembling with emotion and exhaustion. I guess only two or three minutes passed. I was still calming down, getting my head together, getting my head back in touch with my body.

From out of the night came a loud knocking. It thundered through the empty house. It was like a bolt of lightning running down my back. I felt like my spine had fused, and I wouldn't be able to move. Even when I heard the voice it took a few moments to realize who it was.

"Winter! Are you there?"

"Yeah, yeah, hang on."

I got the light on again and padded to the door on cold feet.

Ralph was standing there with a pile of bedding. "I thought you might need these."

"Oh, thanks. Thanks heaps." I think he wanted to bring them in but I took them from him. "That's really nice of you," I said, glad he had given me a chance to show that I wasn't always the super-bitch from hell.

"Oh well. Can't have you sleeping on a bare mattress. Now that the nights are getting a bit cooler."

"Yeah, I've got about three layers of clothes on. But these'll be much better."

Neither of us knew where to go from there.

"Well," Ralph finally said. "We'll have a chat in the morning maybe. Sort things out a bit."

"Yeah, sure. Sounds good."

"And just come up for breakfast anytime you feel like it."

"Oh, yeah, OK."

It was a relief to spread the sheets and doona out, to have a proper pillow, to be able to snuggle under the covers and feel the warmth gradually smother me.

I closed my eyes. As I did I felt the familiar prickling in the corner of each eye. How many times had I gone to sleep like this? How many times had I cried myself to sleep at the Robinsons'? At least this time I wasn't crying from frustration. This time was different. I just felt exhausted. It was like I'd come to the end of a long journey. I'd gone through so much to be here. I'm sure the Robinsons would think it was a pretty bad joke to hear me say that. "We're the ones who've been through the hard time. That little miss has made our lives hell."

But they never knew about those nights I went to sleep with my pillow damp from the silent tears. They never knew about the misery of feeling so far from home, alone among strangers. They never knew how I hungered to be back at Warriewood.

And now I was home. I knew this wasn't the end of my struggles, the end of my search, but here at least there was a chance of reaching it. Living at the Robinsons', I might as well have been on the moon for all the hope I had of finding the answers I wanted.

I don't know how long I stayed awake. It was strange. The house, empty of people and furniture and life, felt more alive than any other house I'd been in. More alive than the Robinsons'. More alive than Ralph and Sylvia's. More alive than my Adelaide grandparents'.

I wondered as I lay there if maybe this house would only feel alive to me. Maybe to anyone else it would be more like a museum. A graveyard. Maybe this house came awake for only one person on earth. Maybe it had been waiting for me all this time.

Gradually the feelings got more specific. At first I'd been looking at a painting from a distance. Now I was close to it, seeing the brightly colored people, the warm petunias in a blue vase, the flames of the fire. I could hear the little sounds people make as they go from room to room. The shush of clothes against a door. The scrape of a foot on the floor. The push of air as someone moves along the corridor. Then the murmur of voices. A cough, a rustle of newspaper, the clink of a coffee cup.

The voices were the most tantalizing. I couldn't quite hear what they were saying. I couldn't distinguish a single word. It sounded like adults, the kind of conversation between people who've known each other a long time. A comfortable, easy conversation. A couple of comments, then silence for a while, then a few more sentences. I wanted to get up and join them. But I knew what would happen if I did. Suddenly I knew, with the certainty of memory. A great tingle ran through my body as my mind and my ears played out the scene.

Dad would say, "Hello, young lady. I thought you were meant to be in bed."

"I'm thirsty," I said.

"That's not very original," Mum said. "Stay there,

Phillip. I'll get it. Now, Winter, one little drink of water and then straight back to bed, OK?"

All those times I'd cried myself to sleep at the Robinsons', it had been a kind of stifled sobbing. I never wanted to be caught. So the tears had seeped out like they were from a tap turned off hard, but still leaking slowly, reluctantly.

Now I cried in a new way. I cried without restraint. I wept like a four-year-old, for the parents I'd lost, for the years I'd been without them, for the parents I'd never see again. My life stretched in front of me, and it looked lonely.

Yet at the same time I knew there was nowhere else on earth I wanted to be. Here at Warriewood was as much comfort as I could hope for. To be in this house, in my own bed, in my own bedroom, to hear those sounds and to feel the live presence of my family from years ago, was like being held close in my mother's arms. That could never happen again in my lifetime, but to have this hint of it, this reminder, seemed to take me back to a time that for twelve years had been beyond the edge of my consciousness, beyond the territory in which I had been living.

CHAPTER THREE

LUCKY IT WAS A BEAUTIFUL morning when I woke up. Otherwise I might have been a bit discouraged by the bare walls and dusty floors of the house. But I pushed the hair out of my eyes and went to the bathroom to check for hot water. I could have saved myself a walk. It was stone motherless cold.

The time was around 6:45. I pulled on some old army trousers and a sweatshirt that we printed for the boarding-house revue at the end of last year. Then I went through the front door and down the hill, across the drive I'd come up last night with Ralph. The old fountain was still there but I thought there'd been a statue of a lady on it, a lady with an umbrella. She'd gone now, maybe folded her umbrella and snuck away to a new home, with a kid who would splash around her feet and look for tadpoles between her legs.

The creek was lined with ferns but most of them were smothered by blackberries. There were so many blackberries I couldn't get close to the water, the babbling, burbling, gurgling, frothing water. But I found a path on the other side and followed that. It was over-grown too, but I picked my way around the fallen logs and bushes of weeds.

The whole time I had music playing for me: the soft yodeling of the creek. Gradually I felt that this was my real welcome home. The creek was saying, "It's good you're back, Winter. We've missed you. This is where you belong."

After maybe a kilometer the little walking track seemed to peter out. A long section had been washed away and then it seemed to get lost among more blackberries. Only a few meters to the left though was a vehicle track, a narrow dirt road running parallel to the creek. So I got onto that and kept walking, thinking: *Guess I should go back pretty soon.*

But it was such a nice morning. After a while I started singing a song I'd just learned from my old singing teacher, Mrs. Scanelli.

Been traveling for miles, I'm lonely,
Looking ahead all the time,
I don't have a map but I'm only
Afraid of looking behind.
And I know that around the next corner,
Somewhere quite close in my life,
In the dark, my future lies waiting,
If I've got a strong enough light.

When I sing I feel like nothing else exists. Just the words and the music and my voice and me. It was like that, walking along the track, helped by the fact that I didn't have to watch where I put my feet, as the road got wider and smoother.

I was singing "Traveling" a second time and had just started the second verse when I got rudely interrupted. I suppose above the murmur of the creek and the sound of my own voice it would have been hard to hear anything, and the way the track zigzagged through thick scrub helped muffle other noises.

Anyway, whatever the reason, I didn't know anyone was coming towards me until the last second. And I mean literally the last second. It was seriously dangerous. Suddenly there was a major assault on my senses. A clatter of hoofs, a snorting of horse's breath, the sight of a huge animal and rider looming over me, even the horse smell filling my nostrils.

I dived off the track to the right, doing a kind of clumsy sprawl down the bank towards the creek, and lay there for a moment on my stomach, face half buried in mud, trying to get my breath.

When I did get it back I was angry. Like, furious. I struggled to my feet and climbed the bank again, onto the track. The rider had managed to pull the horse up and was now swinging him round in a little clearing thirty or forty meters away. He was coming back towards me. I waited with my heart pounding and anger rising like mercury in a melting thermometer. This thermometer knew no maximum. It had gone through two hundred and was still rising when he stopped his horse right in front of me.

"What the hell do you think you're doing?" I yelled. "Don't you know this is private property?"

He nodded. "Yes, I know that."

"So by what God-given right do you think you can come galloping through here like a bloody lunatic on some out-of-control old nag?"

"Old nag's a bit harsh," he said.

He was lucky I didn't have a branch handy, or a large rock. Or a missile launcher.

"Listen," I said, coldly as I could, "get yourself and your horse off this property and don't ever come back."

He stared at me then, his mouth opening a little and his face flushing. He was a good-looking guy, not much older than me, black hair and dark eyes, and a strong chin. The horse wasn't bad either. It was true, "old nag" had been harsh. He was a beautifully groomed chestnut, about eighteen hands, but with wild eyes. The boy must be a pretty good rider, I thought reluctantly, to handle a horse who looked just a little like a natural born killer.

"I bet I know who you are," he said slowly. "You're Winter. Winter De Salis."

"You got that right," I answered, even more coldly. "Now get off my land."

The horse snorted and danced a little, tossing his head. "Hey, Hutch, settle down," the boy said. To me he said: "I heard you were wanting to come back. Are you here for good?"

I couldn't believe the way he was acting. He wasn't taking the slightest notice of what I said, like he owned the place.

"Look," I said, "I don't care what permission you might have from Ralph or anyone else, but I'm telling you now, all deals are off. Don't come on this place again. I won't have people galloping their horses through here any time they feel like it."

He waved back over his shoulder. "Do you remember passing a bridge across the creek, back there a couple of hundred meters?" he asked.

I had noticed a narrow wooden bridge, where the track forked, but I'd come this way, thinking it looked more attractive.

"So?" I asked.

"That's your boundary," he said. "There's a fence up to the left but you can't see it from the track. So it is a bit hard to tell. You're on our land here. But you're welcome. Enjoy your walk."

He clucked at the horse, who was all too keen to get moving, especially now he was facing home again. I had to get out of their way for the second time. I stood there with my face red hot. Any hotter and it would have spontaneously combusted. I watched them, the horse cantering briskly, the boy well balanced on his back, till they were out of sight.

I was just as angry as I had been before, but now it was for a different reason. I hated him for making a fool out of me, for stringing me along like that. And I hated myself for letting it happen.

CHAPTER FOUR

I'D HARDLY FINISHED BREAKFAST when Mr. Carruthers arrived. I'd been expecting him but not quite that quickly. I was taking my second-last mouthful of porridge when the bustle of people at the door told me someone new was coming in.

I knew why. Sylvia or Ralph — probably Sylvia — had called him. I could imagine the conversation: "She's being difficult. Worse than difficult. She's being impossible."

I never quite knew about Mr. Carruthers. For as long as I could remember he had been in charge of the estate. Every three months he'd come to see me in Canberra — in recent years anyway — to give me a copy of his report to the court, and to have a chat about the way it was all going. Sometimes Ralph was with him, more often not.

"Any questions?" Mr. Carruthers would ask at the end. It was only in recent years that I'd been able to think of questions. The last two times I'd hit him with so many that he looked horrified. I had a distinct feeling that he liked me better when I was sweet and cute and passive.

No matter what, though, he was always friendly, polite, cheerful, positive. That part was OK. It was just that somehow — I didn't quite know how — I sensed it was a bit false. Like he'd been through a course or something, in how to be positive. You wouldn't know what he was really thinking.

He came towards me now, eyes flashing behind his glasses. "Winter!" he said. "Welcome back. Welcome back to Warriewood. It's been a long time."

That was typical of Mr. Carruthers. He'd fought like hell to stop me leaving the Robinsons, but now that I was here he would act like it had been his idea all along.

"So," he said, drawing up a chair and sitting beside me, "how's it been so far?"

"Fine," I said. "Good."

"I believe you slept in the homestead last night?"

"Yep."

"Goodness me. All on your own? You're braver than I am. Weren't you nervous?"

"No," I said, not bothering to tell him how unalone I'd felt.

"Well now, we can't have you there while the place is in such a poor state. What would you like to do? I know Ralph and Sylvia are very keen for you to stay with them."

No one seemed to have got the message yet. I was back for good.

"Why is the homestead in such a poor state?" I asked, pushing back the empty bowl of porridge.

"Sorry?" he said, gaping at me, his eyes widening behind his glasses, the glasses lifting slightly as his eyebrows went up.

"Why's the homestead such a mess?" I asked. "Holes in the roof. Rotting floorboards on the veranda. Paint peeling off. Why hasn't anyone looked after it?"

"It's a question of priorities," he said, as though he was my housemistress at school, giving the boarders a lecture on keeping the supper area clean and tidy.

"It's the main building on the property. Were you just going to let it fall down?"

"Oh, no, of course not. I didn't realize it was so run down."

Considering he'd raised the subject himself, I thought that was a bit much.

"But Winter," he continued, "if you feel you'd like some work done on the homestead, why then, that can certainly be arranged. There's enough money available in the trust, and as the administrator I'd see renovations as a perfectly legitimate expenditure."

"OK, well can we get the veranda fixed? And the place painted?"

"Certainly."

"And the carpets replaced?"

"Why don't I call a friend of mine, Bruce McGill. He was a good friend of your parents too. He's an architect who specializes in these old places. He can advise you on what it needs."

"OK. Can you call him today? This morning?"

"Well, certainly, yes, I can certainly do that. He's a busy man, but I'm sure we can get him out here for a look. Now, in the meantime, what will we do about your accommodation? I know Jenny, my wife, would be happy to have you come and stay with us if you think —"

"I'm staying in the homestead."

I wished I could have put it more politely, more graciously, but I was tired of these battles, and I didn't know any other way to win them.

"Oh but Winter, really, I —"

"Where did the furniture go? From the homestead?"

"The what? The furniture? Oh I don't know . . . isn't it there anymore? Have you asked Ralph? I imagine it's stored somewhere around the place."

"He said it had all been wrecked."

"Really? Wrecked? Well, I don't know about that. I'll certainly ask him for more details though. That doesn't seem right."

My strategy had worked. By asking him about the furniture I'd distracted him from his attempts to get me out of the homestead.

I got up. "I'm going to sleep in the homestead every night, Mr. Carruthers. But I want a bit more furniture, just any old bits and pieces, while we find out what's happened to the other stuff. And I need to go shopping for food and things. Can you give me a lift into town? And arrange some money, like an account at the supermarket or something?"

The only comment Mr. Carruthers made after that was as we were driving into Christie.

He said: "You're a strong young lady, Winter. You remind me so much of your mother. I'm still not sure what you've got in mind, coming back here like this, but I admire your spirit. I just worry that you'll get lonely, staying in that big old house on your own. That great big house . . . so many memories . . ."

I didn't answer. I wasn't going to tell him the real reason I had returned to Warriewood. I didn't trust anyone with that information.

CHAPTER FIVE

A WEEK PASSED. I SETTLED INTO a kind of routine. I had enough furniture in the homestead to be comfortable. Ralph dragged out odd pieces from sheds and storerooms around the place. It was junk; I doubted if any of it was from the original stuff, but it would do for the time being. I hadn't asked again about my parents' furniture. I was waiting to see if anyone would offer an explanation. It looked like it would be a long wait.

I spent a lot of money, and just sent the bills to Mr. Carruthers. I got a TV and a video, and organized with Austar to install a satellite dish. I had the telephone reconnected, and rang my friends back in Canberra, spending hours updating them on my new life, catching up on theirs.

Mr. McGill, the architect, arrived on Thursday afternoon. He was nice. We walked around the building, inside and out, then he disappeared underneath it for half an hour. He reappeared all muddy and hot, and covered in spiders' webs. Then he got a ladder and went up into the ceiling for another fifteen minutes, coming down all dusty and hot, and with a fresh coat of spiders' webs.

"It's not too bad," he said. "But it hasn't been looked after the way it deserves. It's a fine old home, Indian-bungalow style, best example in the district. I don't know why it's been let go like this."

He went through his notes with me, then gave me a list. "Roof, mostly sound, but some new sheeting needed. New guttering and downpipes all round. Heating, probably gas-ducted'd be best, but we'll get quotes. I imagine you'll want a security system too. I recommend that you get one anyway. Painting of course, inside and out. That'll be twenty thousand dollars right there, minimum. Now the floor. I suggest you take up all this old carpet and chuck it. Have a look over here."

He led me to a corner of the dining room where the carpet had lifted, and peeled it back. "Look what's under this. Very nice Baltic pine. What I'm thinking is, if we get this polished, and you invest in some rugs, it'll give the place a wonderful atmosphere. What do you think?"

"OK, I guess."

"What exactly are your plans? I mean, you can hardly live here on your own. Not at your age."

I needed to talk to someone, and I liked him. So I admitted, "I don't really know yet. I just wanted to come back. Homesickness maybe. There's only one definite thing I want to do. As for the rest, I'm making it up as I go along. Like, when I got here and saw the state of the homestead, I just thought I should fix it up."

"It was a wonderful home when your parents were here. Your mother had a great eye. She was famous for her sense of design. I don't know who painted the place white. Phyllis would have had a fit. She understood colors like no one I've ever met."

"That's weird," I said. "That's pretty much what my art teacher said about me last term."

"So are you going back to school?"

"I suppose. Sometime. Lately I feel like I've outgrown school."

"There's a good high school at Exley."

"I'd like to go to a government school. I've been at private schools since grade one. I got claustrophobic."

We were walking towards his car and I knew if I didn't ask him now he'd be gone before I got another chance. So keeping my voice nice and steady I said: "What were my parents like?"

"Do you remember much about them?"

"Nuh."

"Hmm. Difficult to know where to start. Look, why don't you come over for dinner Saturday night? We can talk then. My daughter'll be there too. She'll be a bit of company for you. Jess is eighteen. If you want, I can pick you up about six-thirty."

35

"Thanks," I said gratefully. "I'd like that."

As he was getting into his Merc he said, "There's lots of other people you could ask. About your parents, I mean. Your neighbors on that side, the Kennedys, they've been there forever, and they were good friends of your mum and dad."

I blushed at the thought. After the encounter with the boy on the horse I didn't want to go near them.

"Who else?"

"There's the Slades, in Christie. And Dr. Li. But ask your aunt. She'll know them all."

"My who?"

"Your aunt. Mrs. Harrison. Your Aunt Rita. Your great-aunt. You know."

It was kind of funny. He was adding information each time, like dealing new cards in a game of black-jack. It was because he could tell by my expression that I didn't have a clue what he was talking about. Actually it wasn't that funny.

He got out of the car again. "You know. At Bannockburn. Just down the road there."

He pointed towards Christie. I remembered noticing the name "Bannockburn" on an impressive white gateway, when Mr. Carruthers drove me into Christie for the shopping.

"I've got an aunt?"

"A great-aunt, yes. You mean you didn't know?"

"The Robinsons told me I didn't have any close relatives except them."

"Who are the Robinsons?"

"Well, Mrs. Robinson's my mother's half-sister. So she's half an aunt."

"And you didn't know about your Great-aunt Rita? That's astonishing. I can't believe no one's told you."

"I can't believe she's never got in touch with me."

"Well I'm pretty surprised myself. But she is eccentric. And strong-minded. Like all the women in your family." He grinned at me. "Mind you, I've only met two of them, and now you. That makes three. But I think I'm pretty safe with my generalization."

Slipping back into the driver's seat, he added, "Maybe you'd better go and introduce yourself to Mrs. Harrison. You could walk it from here."

"Thanks. I might do just that."

"OK. I'll see you Saturday night then, and you can tell me all about it."

CHAPTER SIX

I WENT BACK TO THE HOMESTEAD in a state of confusion. I felt almost . . . frightened. I know that seems ridiculous, when you've just gained a new relative, a new member of your family. But I guess those words didn't have much meaning to me. My "family" only really had one member, and I was it. My last two grandparents, my father's parents, in Adelaide, had died within a year of each other, four years ago. That seemed to be a pattern in our family.

My mother's parents had died yonks ago — as far as I knew: I was suddenly starting to doubt everything I'd been told — and both my parents had been only children themselves, except for my mother's half-sister and half-brother. The Robinsons were officially related to me, but they'd never seemed like "family members" in the way that my friends had families.

I'm not sure why the Robinsons took me in the first place. Sorry for me, I guess. And I was grateful. Seriously grateful. I mean, if they hadn't, where would I have ended up? In some sort of orphanage? Did they still have places like that? I had a feeling that most kids with no families were fostered out these days. That didn't sound like a great option.

The Robinsons never abused me or anything dramatic. They just seemed indifferent. Maybe that is a kind of abuse. Maybe that's the worst abuse of all. I mean, what would I know? They went on with their lives, almost like they were determined not to let me make any difference to them.

I tiptoed around the house, year after year, thinking that if I made too much noise, if I wore clothes that were too bright and colorful, I wouldn't just disturb the universe, I'd send it spinning into a different dimension.

So I'd adopted my friends' families as mine, kind of, and over the years attached myself to quite a number of their relatives. I spent most of my weekend leaves from boarding school at their places. It had never been a very satisfactory way of getting a family. But beggars can't be choosers, and when it came to rellies I was a beggar.

Sylvia was up at the homestead, fussing around, cleaning the kitchen. I never asked her to do stuff like that, but I wasn't going to stop her either. I mean, I'm a teenager: like I'm really going to tell an adult to stop doing my cleaning for me? A lot of people think I'm crazy, and maybe I am, but I'm not that crazy.

At the same time I wasn't too comfortable about it.

39

There was something irritating . . . a bit unnerving . . . like she was sticking her nose into my territory. Trespassing. Spying on me even. The last thing I wanted was to take her into my confidence. But there was no one else to ask, and besides, she'd lived here so long that it would hardly be news to her that I had a great-aunt.

"Do you know my great-aunt? Mrs. Harrison? Rita Harrison?"

"Sure." She squeezed the mop into the bucket, then paused and looked up at me. "Everyone knows Mrs. Harrison."

"Everyone except me."

"How do you mean?"

"I don't know her. I've never heard of her before. I didn't even know I had an aunt until five minutes ago."

"You didn't? Well, that's strange. I just thought you'd always been in touch. Mind you, she is . . . well, she's a law unto herself. If she decided she didn't want to do something, an army of wild horses couldn't make her. A lot of people around here are terrified of her. She is — what can I say? — a powerful lady."

She started mopping again. "I guess you don't remember too much about your mum and dad?"

"No, not a lot."

"Well, I never met them myself, although I've lived in Christie all my life. Everyone always talked about them though. They were very popular in the district."

"Oh, thanks," I said. I knew she was trying to be

nice, but somehow it didn't quite work. It didn't feel genuine with her. If anything, I felt a bit violated by having her talk about my parents. More trespassing.

"It was a tragedy that they both died. Everyone was devastated. Sometimes life is just so unfair."

"Mmm, I guess so."

I was impatient for her to finish now. I wanted to get the homestead back to myself, so I could think about all this stuff, this news about my great-aunt.

Sylvia carried on, unconcerned. I don't think she was too sensitive to anyone else's feelings.

"I remember my mother coming back from your mother's funeral. She had clay halfway up her shins. It had been raining for weeks, and the ground up there around the lookout is all clay."

I stood there trying to process what she'd said. I could hear my brain going like a computer, when you give it a heap of functions and it makes that clicking sound, as though you're winding up a clockwork toy as fast as you can. Sylvia was mopping away. She hadn't even noticed. I knew I had to say something. Finally I opened my mouth.

"Do you mean my mother's buried near here?"

I suppose the thing that I'd really shocked myself with was the realization that I'd never considered where my parents were buried. How come? I was disgusted that I'd been so thoughtless, and ashamed that I'd never gone looking for their graves.

Sylvia was pretty shocked too. She stood there holding the mop and gaping. Her cheeks, normally so red, were white now, but there was a little burning spot in each one.

"You mean you don't know?"

I was sick of people saying stuff like that to me. I was sick of not knowing anything. I bit my tongue but Sylvia kind of said it for me.

"We keep forgetting that you were so young when it all happened. I'm sorry. I thought you would have known about their graves."

"Well, I don't."

"They're both buried here on the property. Very unusual these days. I don't know how many strings had to be pulled. Must have been a lot of paperwork, I'll bet."

"Where are they buried? Where exactly?"

I had my arms folded tight in front of me, like I was trying to hold myself in, to stop my insides from falling out.

"Why, up at the lookout. Like I said."

"Where's the lookout?"

"Oh, you don't even know . . ."

She leaned the mop against the door frame and took me outside. She pointed towards a gate leading out of the top paddock. "You go through there, and follow the vehicle track to the right. Go up about half a k and take the fork to the left. Just keep going straight on up. It's a good hike, but you can't miss the look-out."

When people give you directions they always finish by saying: "You can't miss it."

Sylvia looked at me anxiously. "Are you going there now? Straight away? You want me to come with you? You sure you'll be all right? It could be a bit hard on you."

"No, I'm fine. It's no big deal. I'm just interested to see it, is all."

I felt her eyes watching me as I walked away across the paddock, but I didn't look round.

CHAPTER SEVEN

SHE WAS RIGHT ABOUT ONE THING: It was quite a hike. The road wound up through open eucalypt forest. I'd been here a couple of times already, earlier in the week, and had wandered off the track down into the fern-lined gullies. But the bush seemed to stretch forever, and before today I hadn't realized it led anywhere definite. I'd assumed it just eventually blended into the next property.

I came to the fork and went on. The road climbed steadily. I got hot and a bit puffed, and took my sweater off and tied it around my waist. This was exactly the sort of exercise Mrs. Scanelli always said I needed, if I wanted to develop my voice. "Big lungs!" she kept telling me. "You need lungs like airbags!" Well, if I kept climbing at this rate I'd soon have them.

I heard a heavy pounding away to my right, in the bush. It'd be a wallaby or kangaroo, escaping from this human trespasser. I strained on tiptoes, trying to see through the thick trees, but there was no sign of it.

The road flattened then started climbing again, at the same time as it swung around further to my right. I could see clear daylight ahead, and a few minutes later found myself at the edge of a firebreak, which ran along either side of a fence line. The break was quite wide, and well mown on the other side, a bit over-grown and wild on this side. I assumed this was the boundary of my property. The road ran parallel to the firebreak, forming one edge of it, and went on up a steep hill to the right.

For a few minutes I'd been subconsciously aware of a buzzing noise, but now that I was in the open it became loud and obvious. I looked across to see where it came from. It was further again to my right, and I was surprised when I turned around to see several hectares of cleared land, the stumps of trees sticking up fresh and raw among the wreckage of the foliage.

A big semi-trailer was parked in the middle of it, with half a load of logs on board. A couple of blokes were working away with chain saws. One of the men looked like Ralph.

I walked across, stepping carefully through the de-bris, past a forklift. It was real ankle-breaking ground. Quite a contrast to the quiet forest I'd just been enjoy-ing.

Neither of the guys had seen or heard me. The closer one was Ralph, as I'd thought. I was only half a dozen steps away when he saw me.

He was lucky he didn't cut his leg off, he got such a shock. The chain saw jerked up then down, and he had to jump away from it to avoid the ugly blade.

"Jesus Christ!" He put it down, turning it off, then removed his ear protectors. "Sorry," he said. He looked white and shaken. "I didn't see you coming. You gave me a shock."

"What are you doing?" I asked.

"Doing? Oh, nothing much. Just, you know, putting in a . . . making the firebreak bigger."

The other bloke had seen me now, and he turned off his chain saw and came over. I'd never seen him before.

"Who are you?" he asked me. He seemed pretty aggressive.

Ralph was anxious to be nice. "This is Winter," he told the man. "Winter De Salis. She's the heir to this property; inherits the place when she turns eighteen. She's just staying here for a while to have a look around."

"Oh yeah, right," the man said. Or grunted. He didn't look too impressed. He didn't look easy to impress. Ralph seemed anxious to impress him though.

"I've just been telling her," Ralph went on, "how we're extending the firebreak. Make the place safer. You know what bushfires are like. Wipe you out in half an hour."

"Yeah, that's the truth," the other man said. "They're a real bugger, them bushfires."

They both stood there. It seemed a really uncomfortable situation. They looked so uneasy.

"Where are you off to then?" Ralph asked.

"Nowhere. Just up to the lookout."

"Oh yeah, well, you're quite a bit off course. You should have gone left at the fork. You want me to show you?"

"Oh, yes, thanks."

"Up the road there . . . it takes a right at the corner of the fence line. Go a k and a half, turn left, and you'll see the lookout on the right."

"OK. I'll see you later."

"Yeah, sure."

Once again I had the sensation of being watched from behind, as I plodded through the fallen timber and up the road. I didn't hear the chain saws start again until I was well inside the cool forest.

I wasn't surprised that they were so nervous, so guarded. Why wouldn't they be? I hate being treated like an idiot. I know when people are lying to me — after all, I've had enough experience of it — and I knew Ralph and his mate were lying through their teeth.

CHAPTER EIGHT

THE LOOKOUT WAS A SURPRISE. Someone, a long time ago, had put a lot of work into building it. A whole section of cliff had been reinforced and built up by rocks in a way that looked natural but must have taken a few people a few months. From the top you could see glimpses of the plains stretching away into the distance beyond Christie, but they were only glimpses, because the trees had grown so high they blocked most of the view.

I did stand and look at the view for a couple of minutes. That might seem pretty strange, considering that for the first time in twelve years I was about to come close to my parents. But I was too nervous. I didn't know if I had as much courage as I thought. This hadn't been part of my plans when I came back to Warriewood. Face it, I hadn't even known that this place, the lookout, existed until an hour and a half before. I certainly hadn't known the graves were there.

Yet a strange thing happened. When I turned away from the view to look for the graves, I knew exactly where they were. I headed off to the right, at about a 45-degree angle from the lookout, and went up a small rise, through scrub and grass and matted under-growth. In a little clearing at the highest point I found them.

My parents lay under a huge blackwood wattle, its dark trunk like a column of mourning. The graves themselves were covered with weeds and fallen bark and dead sticks. I wouldn't have minded if they were covered with native plants and little wildflowers. But they weren't. These weeds were prickly and ugly. At the end of each grave was a headstone. I cleared the grass away from the left-hand one and read the faded words. It said: *In loving memory of Phillip Edward De Salis, born May 15 1945, died by drowning, December 27 1988. The Lord giveth and the Lord taketh away.*

It was the first time I'd known the date of their deaths. That was one of the things I'd returned to War-riewood to find out.

I cleared the other headstone. It read: *Sacred to the memory of Phyllis Antonia Rosemary De Salis, born November 12 1945, died July 9 1989.*

There was no Bible verse on this one. Maybe who-ever buried my mother had lost faith in God, with the two of them dying so close together.

I sat back on my heels, feeling a shock travel up my spine and through my scalp. Close together, yes. But not on the same day. Not on the same day.

Not on the same day. My skin kept tingling, like I'd been wired up to something. This wasn't right. This wasn't the way I understood it. Somewhere along the line I'd got things terribly mixed-up.

I moved over to the tree and sat against it, staring at the stone words. Not on the same day. My mother had been alive for more than six months after my father's death. Then she too had died. How had she died? By accident? There was no clue. Only one thing was certain. She hadn't drowned. Otherwise they would have put that on the headstone, to match the first one.

If she hadn't drowned, the story in my mind, the set of facts I'd lived with all these years, was wrong. The story of my life was false. I'd built my life on a story and it was a lie.

In my mind I went through that story again, trying to work out how it could have broken down, how I'd been led onto this dead-end path. My parents had died in a sailing race. They'd been caught in a wild storm, during the Sydney-Hobart yacht race. Swept overboard. The bodies found a day and a half later. That was the truth. That was the story. That's what the Robinsons had said, the few times they'd talked about it.

I knew though that something had always bothered me. Some nagging thought deep in my mind had never been satisfied. Why else would I have been so desperate to come back, so desperate to find out the truth about my parents? I'd felt like I was on a quest.

Oh, sure, I hadn't told myself I was coming back to find out the truth.

But a force stronger than curiosity had brought me back to Warriewood. That thought in my brain had known something was wrong.

I sat there trembling. The worst thing was that my confusion over the dates, over the way they'd died, made it impossible for me to get close to them now. As I'd trudged up the hill towards this spot, I'd imagined some scene out of a Hollywood movie; I'd feel their presence, feel that they were alive again for me, and fall weeping onto their graves. Then I'd be different somehow. I'd be changed. I'd come down from the hill a new person.

But all I was now was confused. I would come here again. And I would bring stuff to clean the graves. I would care for them, look after them, show my parents that they were loved. But before I came back, I had to know. When I went down to the rest of the world, I'd find out the true story. My life would be on hold until I could solve this mystery.

CHAPTER NINE

B ACK AT THE HOMESTEAD I STILL couldn't find the courage to go visit Mrs. Harrison. I was having enough trouble just finding the courage to think of her as Aunt Rita. I mean, what do you call a great-aunt anyway? All I knew about great-aunts came from a story I remembered Ailsa, my friend at school, telling me: how when she was a little tacker her family went to visit a great-aunt in Mount Isa, and Ailsa somehow got the idea that great-aunt meant great big aunt, so she thought her aunt was a giant. All the way to Mount Isa she was excited, expecting to meet an aunt five meters tall. She was tragically disappointed when they introduced her to a shrunken little old lady.

Maybe that silly story had lodged itself somewhere inside my head, because I think from the moment I heard about Mrs. Harrison from Bruce McGill she started to grow bigger and bigger to me. The way Mr. McGill talked about her, then the way Sylvia talked about her . . . it sounded like she had them both a bit nervous.

Ever since I'd started my campaign to return to Warriewood, I'd felt I was running on my own fuel, with no one around who I could trust to fill my tank. These last few days I was down to my reserves, with no sign of a new supply on the horizon.

So I chickened out from visiting Mrs. Harrison. I told myself that I was exhausted from the walk to the lookout, too tired for the long hike to her place. Instead I decided to start playing detective in earnest.

First I rang Mr. Carruthers' secretary and asked if he could come to Warriewood tomorrow. She said she'd check and call me back.

Then I set myself up for some serious research. I had my notebook computer, and for the first time since the telephone lines were reconnected, I hooked up to my e-mail provider. I nearly fell over when I found forty-eight messages waiting. Maybe I was more popular than I realized. Maybe they were all junk mail. Whatever, I downloaded them without opening them, then switched to the Internet and clicked onto the search engine.

Like with most Internet searches, I spent quite a while chasing shadows. I was scrolling through newspaper archives, concentrating on one date, July 9, 1989. It was a bit of a long shot. If she'd died in a car accident, for example, there might have been only one or two mentions of her name. Forget the one or two.

There might have been no mention at all. Quite often newspapers just say things like "the name has not been released."

On the other hand, according to Bruce McGill, she had been well known in the district. And I knew from the souvenirs I had of my parents that she'd been a star in two areas at least: shooting and horse riding. She'd held two Australian records for marksmanship, and won the Garryowen three times at the Royal Melbourne Show. They call it the Garryowen so people will remember a woman who died trying to save her horse, Garryowen, from a stable fire, and it's the most prestigious riding event in Australia. So that should have been worth a paragraph when she died.

Eventually I connected with the *Age* for 1989. But it seemed like only the major stories for the year were available. I searched for her name, but with no success. Perhaps she hadn't died in the kind of spectacular accident that made the front pages of the papers, like a plane crash.

I realized that my best hope lay in the death notices, the little classified ads that people put in when someone dies. I'd been leaving them for last, because I knew they don't give many details. A lot of them give no details at all. But I opened them for July 9.

Nothing. Nothing. It was as though she hadn't existed. I sat staring at the screen, dumbfounded. Why wouldn't there be a death notice?

Then, just as I was about to give up and discon-
nect, I realized how stupid I was. If she had died on
July 9 there wouldn't have been a death notice on July
9. At best it wouldn't go in till July 10. Probably not till
July 11.

I tried July 10 and drew a blank. Then hit the jack-
pot.

The first thing I saw was my own name. I guess your
own name always jumps out when you see it in print.
But there it was all right, "loving mother of Winter."

I read the notice with tears in my eyes. For a few
moments I forgot the reason I was on the Internet. All
I cared about was that again, for the second time this
day, I was in touch with my mother, my parents. These
little connections were all I could have, but they were
better than the great silence, the vacuum, that I'd
known for so many years.

De Salis (née Osborne), Phyllis Antonia Rosemary,
of "Warriewood," Christie, (tragically) 9 July,
1989, aged 43 years, cherished wife of Phillip Ed-
ward De Salis (decd), much-loved daughter of Max
and Cecilia Osborne (decd), loving mother of Win-
ter, friend and sister to Una and Bruce Robinson,
and Jeremy and Marcia Osborne, dearly beloved
niece of Rita (Mrs. Dirk Harrison). Darling Phyl,
free forever to ride the green meadows and hills you
loved so much.

There were dozens of other messages, a column and a half altogether. It made me sad to read them.

So much feeling in so few words, such a sense that people liked and cared about her.

But there was nothing concrete, no information. The vague feelings that had brought me home for this search, the sense that something was wrong, that something needed to be explored and understood, hadn't been helped any. All I'd done was run up another bill on the Internet, and leave myself with more unanswered questions. *Tragically?* What did that mean? Her death was tragic all right. I knew that. I didn't need a newspaper to tell me.

CHAPTER TEN

I WENT FOR A WALK TO CLEAR
my head. It had been a day of confusion and com-
plication. A day of strong feelings. I needed an emo-
tional rest.

Instead I ran into more emotions.

I went out the front gates of Warriewood and up
the road towards the T-junction. I just scuffed along
in the dust, kicking a pebble in front of me. At the
T-junction I hesitated, then turned right.

I guess our lives are decided by little moments like
that.

A few hundred meters along the road I heard a
scuffling noise close behind. I turned round. On the
grass verge, coming up quite fast with a grin on his
face, was the boy from the other day, on a horse again,
another big one, a grey this time.

"Hello," he called out, starting to laugh already, no
doubt at the memory of how big a fool I'd made of
myself the first time. "How's it going?"

He came alongside me, slowing the horse to my
pace. For the second time I had to admit that he could

handle a horse. At least this one looked a bit more placid.

"Mmm," I said, through gritted teeth. I wasn't going to give him any encouragement. I wasn't in the mood for some smug self-satisfied guy to show off his equestrian skills. Not to mention his skills in coming on to some girl he didn't even know.

"So, been doing any more trespassing lately?" he asked.

What a wanker, I thought. I really couldn't stand him. I decided to freeze him out by being totally serious and totally polite . . . with maybe just a faint hint of sarcasm. "I'm sorry I was on your land," I said. "I didn't realize. I'll get them to fence it off properly, so I don't make the same mistake again."

"Oh God," he laughed. "Did I sound that bad? I'd hate you to put up any more fences. It's not good for the kangaroos."

I couldn't think of anything to say. He was impossible. I walked along in silence. He kept level with me.

After a while he said, "Do you ride?"

"No."

"Oh, don't you? But your mother won the Garryowen."

If I had ten bucks for every time someone said that to me I'd be able to buy this boy's property and get rid of him altogether.

"Yeah, well, I'm not my mother, in case you hadn't noticed."

"Sorry, yeah, that was a pretty dumb remark."

Damn, I thought. Now he's being sensitive. That's the last thing I can deal with right now.

We walked on another hundred meters, with me feeling more and more that I wasn't coming out of this very well. I mean, I know I'm a king-size bitch, I just generally try to hide it so other people won't realize.

He broke the silence.

"Well," he said, "I'd better be going. I've got three essays due Wednesday and I haven't started any of them. But listen, Winter. I know I played you along a bit the other day, and I'm sorry about that, but you've got to admit, you did ask for it."

He was laughing again, something he seemed physically unable to avoid. Laughing at me, anyway.

He went on: "Anyway it'd be good to get to know you a bit better. I mean, the average age in this district is about ninety-three, and you've just lowered that a bit, thank God. So if you want to meet a few people, well, give me a call maybe? Or even, there's a whole bunch of us going into Exley next Friday to see *Night of the Long Knives*. You'd be welcome. I could give you a lift. Have you got a car?"

"I don't even have a license" I said.

"Oh, OK. What are you, sixteen?"

"Yeah."

"Well, are you interested in the movie? Friday night?"

"I'll give you a call, maybe."

"OK, that's cool."

He lifted up in the saddle to get the horse moving again, but just as he did, I said: "It'd help if I knew your name."

"What? Oh yeah!" He laughed and laughed at that. "Oh, what a pisser. My name's Matthew. Matt Kennedy. The best way to get the phone number is in the Yellow Pages, under Horse Studs. It's easier than trying to remember it now. Or else, take Ralph and Sylvia's number and add three. Theirs ends in five; ours ends in eight."

"OK, thanks," I said.

He gave a casual wave and stirred the horse into a canter. He did that pretty well too. No kicking, nothing dramatic. I don't ride, but I know a bit about it, and I know a good rider from a bad one.

When I saw riders like Matthew I kind of thought I should have a go, wished I could become that good. I knew exactly why I'd never tried of course. I wasn't going to risk being compared to the great Phyllis De Salis. It's hard to beat a legend, especially when the person's dead. Especially when she's your mother.

And yet from out of my collection of dim memories were some definite images of me on a horse. It seemed like it had been an enormous horse, but it probably wasn't. To a four-year-old I bet any horse would look enormous.

As I walked back towards Warriewood I couldn't help thinking about Matthew. Matthew Kennedy. Nice name. It was so annoying, I'd met him twice now and both times he hadn't put a foot wrong. Hadn't said anything sarcastic or aggressive or mean. I was the one who'd taken care of those categories for both of us. He'd been good humored, friendly, good looking. The last one he couldn't take any credit for, but I guess the others he could. He hadn't even minded when I'd been so casual about his invitation for next Friday. The trouble was, he had an unfair advantage being on a horse all the time. It meant he could look down on me too easily. The next time we met, if there was a next time, it would have to be on an equal footing.

CHAPTER ELEVEN

SATURDAY MORNING THERE WAS no sign of Mr. Carruthers and no message from him, which annoyed me. I felt restless, with nothing specific or definite to do, so I decided to take another walk. At this rate I'd never need to go to the gym again.

I knew where I wanted to go, but I also knew it would be an unusual walk; I'd do ninety-nine percent of it and then come home without finishing it off.

Funny how already I was calling Warriewood "home" in my mind, so easily, so comfortably. I'd never called the Robinsons' place home, except as an occasional slip of the tongue.

It was a cold morning. Each day seemed shorter than the one before, with daylight savings ended, and the leaves starting to turn. There was a Japanese maple near the homestead that had gone from green to a rich purply red. I loved looking at its deep beautiful colors against the grey of the autumn sky.

I walked at a pretty good rate, head down most of the time, not noticing much. To be honest, I have to admit I was half listening for the busy brisk sound of a horse's hoofs coming up behind me, but that didn't happen. A few cars went past, and a truck, and I had the feeling I was stared at by some of the drivers. I guessed by now the word had gone around that the De Salis girl was back. Ralph was probably entertaining them at the pub every night with stories of my strange behavior.

It took about thirty-five minutes to get to Great-aunt Rita's front gate. By then I was in a different kind of country. Most of this land was cleared, and every second property seemed to be a horse stud. It was flatter, drier. Just that small drop in altitude must make a big difference in rainfall. I didn't like it down here nearly as much as where I was living.

Bannockburn looked very grand. If I hadn't been put off already by the way people spoke about Aunt Rita, and if I hadn't been put off by my own nervousness of meeting her, then her gates would have done the job quite nicely, thank you very much. There were two big white pillars, and a high white log fence, and a long gravel drive lined with pine trees. I couldn't see the house at the end of the drive, but if it was as impressive as the entrance it must have looked like something out of *Gone with the Wind*.

I snuck inside a few meters and peered further down the driveway. Still couldn't see anything. Damn it, I thought. I'll go up the drive as far as it takes to get a view of the place.

It took about three-quarters of a kilometer. I

couldn't believe it. Great-aunt Rita should have been called Grand-aunt Rita. When I finally did get a glimpse of the house, *Gone with the Wind* seemed pretty close. Only, this looked more British than American. More grey than white. It was a two-story mansion from a century or so ago, built of granite, with a circular driveway around a huge horse chestnut tree.

Everything looked so neat. It was as though the drive had been swept with a nailbrush. Made quite a contrast to Warriewood.

Yet something about it was strangely unappealing. You'd think it'd be everyone's dream home, being so grand and old. And it was beautiful. The trouble was, it seemed lifeless. It lacked heart or soul or something. The doors were all closed, the windows were closed, and the ones on the top floor had shutters over them, so they were well and truly sealed up. Matthew said the average age of people in the district was ninety-three; you got the feeling that Great-aunt Rita had done her bit to keep it so high.

I didn't feel any desire to go further up the drive. A relative had been restored to me one day, and I'd lost her the next. Everything I'd heard, and now seen, about Great-aunt Rita convinced me that she was more like one of my dead relatives than my living ones.

CHAPTER TWELVE

I GOT BACK TO WARRIEWOOD just as Mr. Carruthers was leaving. The big brown Landcruiser was coming down the driveway. I leaned against the stone pillar on the left-hand side of the gateway and waited for him. He pulled up beside me and jumped out of the car. It was still a cool day, but the walking had warmed me. I was pretty tired, and a bit lonely and depressed, so even though I never knew whether to trust Mr. Carruthers, I was genuinely pleased to see him. He was always so positive, and always seemed happy to see me; even if it was fake, this time at least I accepted it without question.

"Well, well, well," he said. "I thought I'd missed you."

"You nearly did," I said. "I didn't get any message back from your secretary. So I didn't think you were coming."

"She tried to ring you, but you must have been out. And I was going to Exley anyway, so I thought I'd call in on the off chance. Have you got a few minutes spare?"

He always treated me like that, as though I were

dashing between the Oscar presentations and an urgent appointment with the Prime Minister.

"Sure. You want to come up to the homestead? I've got some good coffee."

"Sounds perfect, Winter. I'll give you a lift."

When we were sitting around the Laminex kitchen table with its bent leg, and Mr. Carruthers had his cup of coffee and I had a Diet Coke, we got down to business.

"Mr. Carruthers, how did my mother die?"

He put his cup down carefully. Without looking at me he said, "I thought you knew that."

"The Robinsons said she'd died in the same accident as my father. In the Sydney-Hobart."

"Yes, they told me they'd said that. But it's not actually correct. She died six months later."

He gazed out the window, at the magpies on the lawn. "I was sorry the Robinsons told you such a story. I did say to them that I couldn't see the point, but once they'd done it, it seemed better to leave things as they were rather than confuse you any further."

"So why didn't they tell me the truth?"

"I honestly don't know. I think they are people who like things neat and tidy, and it seemed to them the neatest and tidiest solution. Maybe they thought it would avoid having to deal with a lot of questions, questions they didn't want to answer. Of course, all it meant was that sooner or later you'd ask the questions

66

anyway, and it would be messier because of the wrong information they'd given you. Which is exactly what's happening now, I suppose."

"So how did she die? Is it something awful? Something to be ashamed of?"

"No no, not at all."

I watched him suspiciously, not sure whether he was being honest. He still wasn't looking at me much, but that might have been his nervousness at dealing with my questions.

"Well?"

"Ralph tells me you went up to see the graves yesterday."

Trust Mr. Carruthers to know everything I'd done.

"Yes, that's how I know she died much later. But I still want to know how."

"Well, Winter, it was an accident. It appears she was having some shooting practice. I assume you know she was an outstanding marksman, er, markswoman. She'd left a rifle near a vehicle, I think, and a dog knocked it down or something, and it went off. My memory's a bit hazy on the details. It was so long ago. But I remember she was killed instantly."

I sat there dumbfounded. I couldn't believe it. And soon, as I sat there, it dawned on me that I truly couldn't believe it. Literally.

"What was she doing leaving a loaded rifle lying around?"

"Oh, I don't know. I suppose it's the kind of thing people do."

"But I've been living in the city twelve years and even I know you don't leave a loaded rifle anywhere. It's like, it's like . . ." I searched my mind for a good comparison. "It's like drunk driving. It's like going through a red light. It's like throwing petrol on a fire. And my mother was an expert shot. There's no way in the world she'd have done something so stupid."

Mr. Carruthers leaned forward earnestly. "On the contrary, Winter. That's exactly how these things happen. They always happen to people like your mother. The people who are overconfident. They're the ones most at risk. They forget that even they can get hurt."

He seemed terribly anxious to convince me. He'd just said the same thing about four different times, to drive home the point.

I didn't know what else to say. I didn't know whether I was on the right track, or whether I just wanted to believe such an accident couldn't have happened. I know I was really shocked and upset by the thought of her dying like that. I got the shakes, and had to grip myself to stop the shivering.

After a while I got better self-control. To change the subject completely, I asked Mr. Carruthers: "How much do Ralph and Sylvia get paid?"

He looked at me in amazement. "I'm sorry?"

"How much are they paid? Out of the estate?"

"Well, it's on the statement to the court. The statements I've been supplying you with for the last few years. Just give me a minute . . . I'll see if I've got one."

He rummaged in his briefcase. I'd never seen him so off balance. As he searched, he asked me: "May I inquire why you've become interested in their wages? You don't have to answer, of course, but I'm curious."

"I was just wondering."

I knew that answer wouldn't give him much satisfaction.

He pulled out a red folder with the words *Warriewood Estate* on the cover and opened it briskly.

"Hmm, let's have a look. . . . last financial year, counting super, $55,914. Say, fifty-six thousand."

"Plus the house?"

"I'm sorry?"

I knew he hated these kinds of questions.

"Do they pay any rent for the house?"

"Ah, no, I don't believe they do."

"Any other freebies?"

"Well, the estate pays their water and electricity. I think that's partly because all the water comes through one meter, so you can't divide the manager's use from the rest of the buildings."

"Have you noticed anything about this property?"

"Er, what exactly did you have in mind?"

Suddenly all the frustration and anger that had been building up in me since I arrived — before I arrived, even — detonated.

"These people are getting a thousand bucks a week, and then some, and look at the place! Just look at it! There are so many blackberries along the creek you can't even get to the water. The major crop on this property is blackberries! They're everywhere. The gardens are full of some disgusting bloody sticky weed that clings so close you need a microsurgeon to get it off. You go for a walk in any direction and if the path isn't smothered by weeds it's washed away by erosion. There are gullies up the back that are going to be like the Grand Canyon in a few more years. Half the fences are falling down, the gutters are full of leaves and crap, the drains are blocked so tight that for any water to get through it has to have a passport. And as for my parents' graves! Jeez! Another couple of years and I wouldn't have even found them. Then there's this —"

"I can understand you being upset about the graves," Mr. Carruthers interrupted, smooth as ever.

Well, I thought, you won't be smooth much longer. But I kept talking, ignoring his comment.

"This house, the homestead. Look at it! Look around you! I've already told you what I think about that. But what about the furniture? My parents' furniture. Ralph tells me some bullshit story about borers and water through the ceiling! Does he honestly expect me to believe that? How stupid does he think I am? A whole houseful of furniture disappears! Beds, wardrobes, tables, chairs. I've seen the photos. I know what it was like. It was good stuff, beautiful stuff. My parents had taste. They filled this house with antiques. And the whole bloody lot's gone. They must have —"

"Wait," Mr. Carruthers interrupted again. He was getting nervous now. "I'm sure that whatever else Ralph and Sylvia are, they're honest. I don't think you can accuse them of . . . they wouldn't . . ."

"Oh yeah?" I said. "Tell me this then. How much money has come into this estate in the last few years from the sale of timber?"

"Timber? Timber? There's never been any revenue from that. It's always been a beef operation, as you know, and then there's the remnant vegetation that your parents wouldn't —"

"I've got news for you," I said, as brutally as I could. "Ralph and some mate of his have logged a huge patch of that remnant vegetation up the back there, on the western side. They're trucking the stuff out. I've seen them at work. They had their own semi-trailer and forklift in there yesterday, taking another load. And it's been going on for years. You only have to look at the stumps."

Mr. Carruthers stared at me. In that moment I thought: *Either this guy's fair dinkum, or he's a hell of an actor.*

He said: "I can't believe what you're telling me." He leaned back in his chair. He took off his glasses and stared at me. "Winter, if this has been happening, if this is true, I can only say . . ."

"It's been happening," I said. "It's true."

"As I think you know, the bush on this property is protected. It's under a covenant. It would be entirely illegal for anyone, even you, to be logging . . ."

"Ralph gave me some story about a firebreak. More bullshit. This is no firebreak. They've wiped out a huge area of bush, where I guess they thought they were safe."

"Well, I still don't know what to say. This is a very serious matter. I shall have to speak to Sylvia and Ralph. And perhaps get some other advice. I'd better . . ."

"Yeah," I said. "I want you to speak to Sylvia and Ralph. And I'll tell you what to say. They're fired. Sacked. I want them off this property by five o'clock tonight."

Now, finally, I had him. His jaw went low and his mouth way out of control. He was like a cow chewing his cud, as though he were rolling something around in his mouth, over and over. His neck jerked away as if he had a chicken bone stuck in his throat.

I just waited. I was extremely terrified doing this, sweating like a pig in a sauna, but kind of enjoying it too, in some strange way.

"Winter, you just can't do that," he finally gasped.

"Yes I can."

"No no, it's not like a private matter between you and your relatives or your friends. It's very different. It's so different. There are all kinds of legal matters involved. It'd take quite some time. This has been their home for so long. I'd have to talk to our legal people."

"Look," I said. "I don't care what it takes or what it costs, they're out of here today."

"No no, Winter, you must listen to me."

"Mr. Carruthers," I said, "you're the trustee of this estate. You have been for twelve years. I don't know how the place can have been so neglected while you were in charge. That's a big mystery to me. But in two years, when I turn eighteen — in less than two years — I'll be in charge. In the meantime you can block me on pretty much anything. Or that's how I understand the way it works. But if you block me on this now, the day I turn eighteen will be the last day you have anything to do with Warriewood. If you want to stay on as my financial adviser, you better get those two good-for-nothing crooks out of here by five o'clock."

He went to say something, but I wouldn't let him. I kept talking. I thought I knew him pretty well. I was dead sure that when it came to the crunch, if he had to choose between sacrificing Ralph and Sylvia and sacrificing himself, there was only one way he would jump.

"I suggest you tell them that if they're still here tomorrow I'll have the police in to investigate the theft of my timber and the theft of my furniture. And I'll ring *A Current Affair* and ask them up here, for a story about an orphan who's been ripped off by the people who were meant to be protecting her interests. On the other hand, if Ralph and Sylvia are out by five o'clock they might just get lucky, and avoid seeing their names in the newspapers."

That was all. I'd finished. I'd covered everything I'd thought of, everything I wanted to say. I leaned back in my chair, my hands spread flat on the table so he couldn't see them trembling, and waited.

Finally he said: "I told you the other day you were very like your mother. By God, I was right about that."

He got up. "I'll go and see them now," he said. His voice was subdued. "I'll see what can be done. But, well, if you're absolutely set on this, I suppose I'll have to find a way to make it happen."

CHAPTER THIRTEEN

I DIDN'T PARTICULARLY WANT to see Matthew Kennedy that afternoon, but it just so happened that I went for a walk along the same stretch of road I'd seen him on the day before, and at about the same time. I mean, it's a free country. I can walk where I want, when I want, and if some conceited guy on a horse happens to want to ride there too, well, it's a big country as well as a free one, so I guess there's room for us both.

The main reason I went that way was that despite my courage in dealing with Mr. Carruthers I was so terrified at what I'd done, and what the consequences might be, that I virtually hid for the rest of the day. I desperately didn't want to see Ralph and Sylvia, and if the choice was between them and Matthew Kennedy, I'd settle for Matthew Kennedy.

I knew it was really gutless to leave it all to Mr. Carruthers. I remember hearing some saying once about people who make the bullets but then get other people to fire them. That was me all right. But I felt like I'd done enough for one day. No way could I have handled any more drama.

I'd gone past the point where Matthew had left me the day before, and had just about given up and decided he wasn't coming — not that I cared one way or the other — when I heard a brisk rat-a-tat-tat from behind.

"Winter! G'day!" he said, slowing the horse to walk alongside me. He was on the chestnut again. "How's it going? Ready for a riding lesson?"

"I'm not taking any riding lessons, thanks very much. And certainly not from you."

"You don't know what you're missing. I'll have you know I got third in the under-ten Novice at the Christie Pony Club, a few years back."

"Who was under ten? You or the horse?"

"Well, both of us actually."

We went a bit further, neither of us speaking.

Then Matthew said: "Hey, are you all right? You look kind of stressed."

"Thanks. That's what a girl always likes to hear, that she's looking her absolute best."

Usually he was the one laughing. This time I was trying to put him off by being funny, and he was determined to be serious.

"Hey, you really are upset about something, aren't you?"

"What are you, the school counselor?"

He swung himself off the horse, without even stopping him properly, which seemed pretty impressive. Holding the reins, Matthew walked alongside me,

76

peering closely at my face. I'd forgotten that this was what I'd wanted, to meet him on equal terms. All I could think was how terrible I must look.

But I had to say something. So I told him: "I just sacked Sylvia and Ralph."

I think apart from anything else I wanted reassurance that I'd done the right thing, that I hadn't made some horrible mistake and turned a couple of aging and devoted servants out into the harsh winter. I was scared that Sylvia and Ralph might be the most popular people in the district.

Matthew buckled at the knees. Only for a moment, but he really did stagger. Then he recovered. Slightly.

"You what?"

"You heard me."

"You sacked Sylvia and Ralph?"

I didn't answer.

"All by yourself? What, you just went up to them and said, 'You're fired, get out'?"

"I got the trustee to do it."

"I can't believe it. My God, you really are something. The other day, when you went for me on that track through the bush, I thought, 'Wow, this girl is running on nuclear power.' I was right about that. My God. You sacked Sylvia and Ralph. This is the most amazing thing I've ever heard. They've been there ten years. You've been here three days and you sack them. Wait till I tell Dad."

"It's a bit more than three days."

"What, four days?"

"No, no way. Give me a break. It's a couple of weeks."

We both started laughing then. Suddenly we were both having absolute spaz attacks. We kept walking but we were in hysterics for about a hundred meters. Eventually we calmed down. Matthew took off his helmet and wiped his face.

"So, am I the biggest bitch in the district?" I asked. "Is everyone going to hate me?"

"Are you kidding? For sacking Sylvia and Ralph? Those two are the biggest crooks I've ever seen. They've been robbing Warriewood blind, from the day they started there. No one's going to hate you for giving them the shaft. You'll get a standing ovation from here to Christie."

It was my turn to buckle at the knees. Such a tidal wave of relief hit me that it's lucky it didn't knock me over. Although Mr. Carruthers probably thought I had no idea, I knew what a major thing it is to give someone the sack. Especially when they lose their house as well. We'd watched *Tree of Wooden Clogs* in Italian classes at school. I didn't want to be one of those old-style property owners, treating employees like they were markers on a Monopoly board.

"Listen," Matthew said. "You look like you're going to pass out. Why don't you come back to my place?

Have a coffee or something. I mean, it can't be a lot of laughs for you at Warriewood at the moment, with Ralph and Sylvia slinking around probably thinking they'd like to put a wedge between your eyes and then attack it with a large sledgie. How long before they go?"

"Five o'clock," I said, glancing at my watch.

"Five o'clock today? Wow. You really don't mess around. I'd hate to be on your bad side. Lucky we've always gotten on so well."

I blushed at that. I was feeling nothing but embarrassment at the way I'd treated Matthew.

"I don't think I can. Come back to your place, I mean. I'm going out to dinner, at the McGills."

"What time?"

"I think he said he'd pick me up at six-thirty."

"Well, you've got heaps of time. And honestly, you'd be better off at our place until Sylvia and Ralph drive off into the sunset in their brand-new Range Rover."

"I must admit, that Range Rover did bother me a bit. That's what first made me wonder about them. I mean, I don't know much about cars, but I think they're at least a hundred thousand bucks."

"Yeah. Worth almost as much as Hutch here." He patted the horse's neck as we turned around and started back.

"Is he worth a lot?"

"Yeah. But not as much as he thinks he is."

"He's a beautiful horse. And you've got him in such good nick."

"Thanks."

"But I wouldn't like to get on his bad side either."

"No." He looked at me with new interest. "Hey, for someone who doesn't ride, you're a pretty good judge. Maybe you have got your mother's eye."

"What do you do with your horses? Breed them? You said you had a stud. Do you race them?"

"Yeah, both. Hutch's the racecourse star. He's won two Group Ones. The Summer Cup and the Memsie Stakes. He's going back into training next week. No more nice bushwalks for you, you big bludger," he said, giving the chestnut flank a slap. Hutch didn't seem too bothered, just rolled one eye at Matthew, and trotted on briskly. Maybe he was thinking of home, and a bucket of oats. I noticed Matthew kept him on the road side, so he couldn't go for the grass.

"So anyway," Matthew continued, "what do you think? Come home and then I can take you back about six o'clock. By then Ralph and Sylvia should be out of the way. Or, better still, we can ring Mr. McGill and get him to pick you up from our place. That way you won't have to go to Warriewood at all."

"Are you kidding? Go out to dinner in this stuff?" I waved a hand at my daggy dusty khaki cargo pants. "But thanks, it would be nice to go to your place. I can walk home from there, and get changed. If I leave by five-thirty, it should be fine."

"Well, the only thing is . . ." He hesitated. "The thing is, I'd rather take you. Because, face it, if Sylvia and Ralph are still there, and they turn nasty, it could get rough. Imagine if you walk in your front door and find them trashing the place. Writing 'Winter Sux' all over your walls."

"Short-sheeting my bed."

"Exactly. See what I mean? It could even get that ugly."

It was my turn to hesitate. Being looked after was an unfamiliar experience. I wasn't sure if I liked it. Gradually, living in Canberra, I'd learned to fight every fight by myself, to fly solo. On the other hand, the idea of facing Sylvia and Ralph alone, at dusk, in that big empty house, was genuinely scary.

"OK, thanks," I said, privately wondering what the Robinsons would say if they heard that voice coming out of my mouth. That soft, grateful voice. They probably would have looked for the ventriloquist.

"Look," Matthew said, putting his helmet on. "I'd better give this big lazy lug a bit of a gallop or he'll kick the place down tonight. Do you know where our front gate is?"

"Yeah."

"OK. So if you come in there, I'll have him rubbed

down and I'll be waiting at the top of the drive. Is that OK?"

"Sure. See you then. Oh . . . and . . . thanks, OK?"

He waved casually and swung himself up onto Hutch, gathered in the reins and cluck-clucked the horse into a canter. When he remounted Hutch I'd been struck again by how big a horse he was. He looked as high as a garage.

I walked on, feeling a little better. Feeling quite a lot better actually. I did a mental search through my repertoire of songs, trying to find something. Eventually I found one.

When you're out there in the nowhere,
And it's getting kind of rough,
Don't be worried, don't be lonely,
Don't forget that love's enough.

Love's the answer, not the question
Love's the reason for your life . . .

CHAPTER FOURTEEN

MATTHEW'S FATHER WAS THE funniest, most cheerful man I'd ever met. Everything was a joke to him. When I followed Matthew into their kitchen, Mr. Kennedy jumped to his feet, picked me up in two enormous arms, and gave me a huge hug.

"Fantastic!" he boomed. "Fantastic! Truly you are a De Salis! I've been trying to get rid of those two parasites for years, and you do it in a fortnight. How old are you?"

"Sixteen."

"Fantastic. When I was sixteen I modeled myself on my guinea pig. Hid in my pen and shut up. My God, you'll be running the country in another twelve months. Do you want a coffee? You probably live on rum and milk."

"Coffee'd be nice, thanks," I said. I liked him instantly, but I feel shy around people who are so extroverted.

"So how did you get onto the wicked Sylvia's little rackets?" he asked. "Found a printing press in the cellar, did you? Churning out hundred-dollar notes by the truckful? Or were they respraying luxury cars in the barn?"

"Ralph's cleared a big area of timber, halfway up to the lookout," I said. "He had a mate with him and they were loading it onto a semitrailer."

"Did he, by Jove? They must have thought they could get away with anything. You know, I employed Ralph for a while, years ago, before he and Sylvia got the job on Warriewood. Every time I came back from an interstate trip I'd find another five hundred k's on the Merc. I think he was running a taxi service for his mates. Sylvia's the brains behind their little capers though. Ralph isn't smart enough. He'd have trouble chewing gum while he walked. I mean, speak no ill of the dead or departed, but those two were the Bonnie and Clyde of Christie."

He poured me a coffee.

"But that's terrible about your timber. We take care of our bush around here. There's precious little of it left. If you like I'll come up with you and have a look. We'll see what we can do about regenerating it."

"Thanks," I said, "I'd appreciate that."

"It's the least I can do for the daughter of Phillip and Phyllis."

"Did you know them well?"

"Oh yes. Knew 'em and loved 'em. They were special. They were Hall of Fame neighbors."

"Is it true my mother died in a shooting accident?"

"Why yes."

But again his good humor seemed to fade, and he looked troubled, as he had when I told him about the logging of the bush.

"How?"

"Well, one of her dogs knocked a loaded rifle. I don't know whether she even had the safety catch on, but of course safeties are a mechanical operation, and they're not reliable anyway."

"That's why Dad's told me a hundred times not to have a bullet in the magazine until I'm ready to fire," Matthew said, pushing a plate of choc-chip cookies towards me. "He always quotes what happened to your mother as the reason."

"But how could she have done something so thoughtless," I asked, "with her experience?"

Mr. Kennedy shook his head. "I don't know. I honestly don't know. I've asked myself the same question many times. All I can think is that she was so devastated by Phillip's death that she wasn't herself, wasn't thinking straight."

"So she was still very upset, all those months later?"

"Well, yes, almost more upset than when she got the news. At first she kept saying she could accept it because Phillip died doing something he loved, he

85

died in the way he would have wanted. Not that he wanted to die of course. There never was anyone more full of life. But you know what I mean.

"Anyway, as the months went on I think she started to realize what his death meant. The loss of his friendship, his company; the end of their relationship. No father for their little daughter. The loneliness was getting to her. So I don't know if she was concentrating too well."

"Was I there when it happened? Like, on the spot?"

"Do you know, I'm not sure. I doubt it, because I think I would have heard if you were. You know how people talk. There would have been a lot of comment about how terrible it was that her little daughter saw the whole thing . . ."

He paused and looked at me anxiously, obviously worried he might be upsetting me. But I was calm enough. I wanted to know, that was the main thing.

"You think she was really depressed then?"

For the first time he realized where I was going with this. His mouth opened for a moment and he put down his cup.

"Oh Winter . . . oh dear. I don't know what to say. I don't think it was anything like that. I don't think . . ."

"But there's something," I said. "Something's bugging you. You're not happy in your mind about it."

86

Looking away through the window, not to avoid my gaze, but as though he were trying to remember that day so many years ago, he said slowly, "I think it was the way Mrs. Harrison acted. Your aunt. I mean, your great-aunt I suppose she'd be. She was there when it happened. There was something about her, about Mrs. Stone, too . . . of course they were terribly distressed, terribly . . . your great-aunt and Phyllis were very close . . . but still, even so, they just shut down so much. . . ."

"Shut down?"

"Yes. Look, I can't put my finger on it. . . ." He shook his head briskly, as though he wanted to clear away the confusion of his thoughts. "Oh, it was nothing. They were just upset. I'm sorry, I shouldn't be making it worse for you than it is already. Don't take any notice. I'm just an old man having daydreams."

"Who's Mrs. Stone?"

"She was housekeeper for your parents. She works for Mrs. Harrison now."

And that was all I got out of him. A few minutes later I had to say goodbye. It was time for my security guard to escort me home.

CHAPTER FIFTEEN

THE NEXT MORNING I GOT A
sense of what the departure of Ralph and Sylvia
meant in practical terms. Like, really practical terms.
Since I got back I'd done enough work with Ralph to
have a fair idea of the daily routine. I still hadn't
thought about how to replace him — didn't have a
clue — but I figured that in the short term I could
keep the place going OK. I got up at seven-fifteen and
by a quarter to eight I was outside and ready to work.

The first stuff was easy. Most of the cattle were in
good paddocks, but there were three paddocks where
Ralph had been hand feeding. I got the biggest wheel-
barrow from the barn and dropped a couple of bales
into two paddocks and one into the third, where there
were only four cows with their calves. There was
something very satisfying about it. They got so excited
when they saw me coming. All the bellowing and
grunting and groaning — it reminded me of boarding
school in Canberra. They nuzzled the bales so enthu-
siastically that they knocked over the barrow. I almost
had to push them away so I could cut the twine. In the
last paddock I actually lost the twine. The trouble was

that the twine was the same color as the hay, and when it dropped in among the hay on the ground I couldn't see it at all. At first it was a joke, but after a while I started getting seriously worried. The cattle were munching away with such speed and sheer happiness that I could imagine the twine disappearing down their throats as quickly as the hay. I was combing around on the ground, getting cattle shit on my hands, and cursing the idiot who had tied those bales with yellow twine. I found one length of the stuff, but then a moment later was sure I saw the other one going down the throat of one of the cows, like an Italian momma eating spaghetti. I grabbed for it but all I did was alarm her. She backed away fast and the last bit of yellow was sucked into her mouth.

Oh no, I thought. *Oh Jeez. What do I do now? Get the vet out? Great start to my career looking after Warriewood.*

Then I decided maybe I was wrong, maybe it wasn't the twine I'd seen, just another length of hay. So I started searching again, and about four minutes later found it.

It wasn't exactly a great thrill, just a relief. I sat back on my heels looking at the cattle and thinking, *I've sure got a lot to learn.*

I went and let the chooks out for their daily graze, threw some wheat around for them, checked their pellets and water, and got the eggs. Only four. Seemed like the chooks were slowing down for winter. I wondered what had happened to the eggs in the past. Guess they were just another perk for Sylvia and Ralph.

Back in the barn I got a mattock and some thick gloves and went out to begin the campaign that had been in the back of my mind — at the front of my mind quite a lot of the time — since I returned to Warriewood. Those bloody blackberries. I hated them from the moment I took my first early morning walk along the creek. I figured it'd probably take ten or twenty years to get rid of them, but I was going to make a start. Every journey begins with a single step.

I knew the easy way would be to do it with poison, but I didn't want that. Maybe just because I'm pig-headed; if there's a difficult way to do something I'll always find it. But I couldn't bear to think of poison washing down into my beautiful creek, killing the trout and the turtles and the platypuses, and even the little insects that skimmed across the water. I felt they trusted me to keep the water safe for them, and I was going to do just that.

So I went at the blackberries with the mattock, digging out the big plants and pulling out the little ones.

I soon realized I was lucky in one way. Because we were well into autumn there'd been a good bit of rain, and the ground was quite soft. So the roots came out easier than I could have expected. The further into the gullies they were, the more easily they came out. Once I got up onto the higher ground, it was hard work. I don't think I got all the roots on any of them, but I had to hope that I was getting enough to stop them making a comeback.

When I got a big one out with most of its root system it was deliciously satisfying, like no other job I've ever done. Some of them were huge. I'd walk back from the gully, dragging the plant with me, and sometimes I'd have to go twenty meters to get it all out from the undergrowth. It was like holding up a huge fish pulled from the bottom of the ocean.

I soon came to realize that blackberries are the most pernicious, evil creations on the face of the planet. They'd crept through the bushes, along the ground, where no one could see them, putting down new little white roots wherever they went. And they hid their roots so cleverly. Some of them were actually growing out of the trunks of tree ferns. Those ones were almost impossible to get out.

And they fought me. They fought tooth and nail, writhing around my legs like tentacles from some ferocious jungle creature. They grabbed me like they wanted to wrap me in barbed wire. They bit and scratched and swore and tore.

All of this made destroying them more satisfying, in spite of the frustrations. Three times I went into tantrum territory, just like I was back in school, or at the Robinsons'. I lost all rational thought each time. I swore and tore right back at the mongrels, ripping them with all my strength, and not stopping till I was hot and sweaty and exhausted.

The good news was that after a couple of hours I could actually see some changes. Some improvement. The big plants covered such huge areas that by removing one blackberry I opened up quite a space. Looking back along the bank of the creek, in among the ferns and hydrangeas and rhodies, I could see grass again. I felt I'd given the garden and lawn room to breathe, room to grow. And I'd done it all myself.

The bad thing was that it got kind of lonely. I wanted someone working with me, so we could swap the odd comment, have a laugh together, hold up a massive blackberry and say, "Hey, look how big mine is," or something equally dumb.

Round about eleven o'clock I threw down the mattock and gloves, staggered to a patch of lawn and flopped onto the grass. I was exhausted. I really wasn't fit enough for this kind of work. It was different from the stuff you do in a gym. I must have been using different muscles or something. I lay there with an arm over my eyes, listening to the sound of the wrens and red-tails and kookaburras, thinking, I must get a dog for company, and wondering again how my mother had really died. Deep down I knew she hadn't been killed in such a stupid dumb accident.

"Winter, hi!" a voice said.

I sat up quickly, looking around. I hate surprises. I hate shocks. I hate anything unexpected.

Standing there was Jessica McGill. At least this was a nice surprise. She had been so much fun at dinner the night before. I'd been quite nervous when I got to her place. Not only because of my post-traumatic stress after the Ralph and Sylvia Show, but also with the lump I get in my stomach when I meet new people. It's like I've swallowed a billiard ball.

With Mr. McGill being an architect I knew they'd have a pretty nice house, and it was nice, but not like those ones that hit you from ten k's away. Not some palace with a pair of white lions guarding the front gate. This was a long low timber place that stretched into the distance to the left and right and had big flower gardens all around. The path leading to the front door was a real obstacle course, with heaps of potted plants and little trees and creepers, and a bronze figure of a girl holding a lamp.

Inside it was comfortable and warm, but I started to realize how big it was, with rooms leading to rooms leading to more rooms. To be honest you'd have to say it was shabby in some ways. The sofas looked like they were out of a dog kennel, and not just because a couple of golden retrievers were snoring away on them. The dogs were so old and lazy they opened one eye each, looked at me, yawned and went back to sleep.

But the sofas were falling apart at the seams, and they could have done with a shampoo. There were cracks in the ceiling, and books and magazines and CDs in piles everywhere.

Funny though, it wasn't a mess. It didn't look grubby or unloved. I don't know how some houses can be like that and some can't. Maybe it was all part of Mr. McGill's architectural genius. Maybe the whole room was carefully planned and he'd paid a fortune to get sofas with that dilapidated look. Maybe not.

Mr. and Mrs. McGill were both there and they were really friendly. I asked for a Diet Coke and of course that turned out to be the only thing they didn't have, so Mr. McGill went off to another room to look for a straight Coke. I headed for the sofas and started slobbering over the dogs. It's what I do when I'm nervous, use dogs as security blankets. The retrievers didn't seem to mind. Mr. McGill came back with a Schweppes Cola, which I hate, but I wasn't about to say that. I remembered my manners and went and helped Mrs. McGill in the kitchen, and that was quite good, because it was easier having something to do, being able to talk while chopping carrots and stirring the sauce.

Jessica had arrived home just in time for dinner. Jessica's one of those people who bounce. She bounced in the front door, like she was running on different batteries from the rest of us. The dogs actually dragged themselves off the sofas to greet her. I was impressed by that. I was impressed by the relationship she had with her parents too. Right away she launched into a big conversation about her flute teacher and how he wanted her to get a new flute and it was going to cost some amazing amount of money, two thousand dollars I think. Instead of her parents going "No way, you've got to be joking," they took it pretty well, asking about where it was made and stuff, and instead of Jessica going off her head and yelling "Either I get a new flute or I'm out of here," she was like "But I don't really know whether I need it — I'm going to ask a few more people on Monday."

She's doing a music course at the College of the Arts, majoring in flute and harp. At dinner she started telling us about her trip home, and how a group of them started singing *a capella* on the tram on their way to the station and the driver stopped the tram and ordered them off and the passengers booed the driver, but he wouldn't back down, so Jess and her mates got off the tram singing "You've Lost that Loving Feeling" at the driver while the passengers all cheered.

So the next thing Jess and I are singing "You've Lost that Loving Feeling," and then we discover we both love Kasey Chambers, so we get into the whole Kasey Chambers songbook, starting with "The Captain" and going on to "This Flower," and then Mrs. McGill brings out the nasi goreng.

It's a bit hard to sing with your mouth full of rice.

"All the music you kids listen to," said Mr. McGill, "it's the same songs we listened to, recycled. What goes around comes around."

"Yeah, right, Dad, you musical legend," Jess said, "like you'd really know what we listen to."

"Well, what's number one on the Top 40 at the moment, for example?"

"Dad!" Jessica speared a prawn with her chopstick and held it up in the air like she'd harpooned it. "What language are you talking? Top 40? We don't talk like that."

"Triple J's Hottest 100, now that's a different matter," I said.

"Yeah, I'm a J girl," Jess agreed.

"OK then, what's a song that's really popular?" Mr. McGill asked. "I bet it'll be a rehash from the sixties or seventies."

"Um, how about 'When Your Baby Says It's Time to Come, You Know It's Time to Go,'" Jess said.

"Jessica!" said Mrs. McGill.

"Oh. I must admit, I haven't heard of that," Mr. McGill said.

"That's because I just made it up."

After dinner Jessica and I spent the rest of the evening in her room, with me singing and Jess switching between harp and flute. We tried making up words for "When Your Baby Says It's Time to Come, You

Know It's Time to Go." It was pretty funny. I wish I'd written them down.

On second thoughts, maybe not. My life's ambition is to be the Princess of Cool, and I don't think I'd have earned many votes with the lyrics I was suggesting.

I loved the whole evening. It was such a relief after all the bad stuff. We hadn't talked about my parents, but I wasn't in the mood anyway.

Mr. McGill drove me home. It was 12:30 before I got to bed. That was good too, because I was so tired I didn't think about being alone on the property: sixteen years old and just me, on six hundred hectares of farmland and bush.

But I felt a flush of delight to see Jessica again so soon.

"Hi," I said, jumping up. "How did you get here?"

"I rode over. Wow, look at the blackberries. Have you pulled all these out this morning?"

"You wanna see my scars?"

"My God, Winter, you really are serious about this."

I just shrugged, but I was pleased with her praise. After all, she was two years older than me.

"You want a hand?"

"Are you kidding? No, I couldn't ask you. It's such sweaty horrible work, and you'll scratch your hands so badly you'll never play harp again."

"I'll take the risk. It looks quite fun actually."

"Well, to be honest it is strangely satisfying."

We walked up to the barn and got another pair of gloves and a spade. On the way back Jess told me her great idea. "I was thinking, do you want someone to come and stay here for a while? 'Cos I'm sick to death of living at home but I can't afford to live anywhere else. And you know how you were saying last night you were finding the house so big and empty . . ."

"Oh wow. That'd be so cool! I'd love it!"

"I wouldn't be here during the day, because of school, but I'd be here nights and weekends."

"That wouldn't matter."

Jess got really warmed up then. She's such a nice person. "And I had another idea, why don't we put an act together and do some busking? If I played flute, or guitar, because I can get by with that too, and you sang, I reckon we'd make a fortune. You've got such a good voice. Some of the kids at school make eighty bucks in two hours busking. But the singers always do the best. We might even get some proper jobs, like in a bar or something."

"Except I'm underage."

"Oh yeah, I forgot that. Well, in a café maybe. There are some good gigs around, if you know where to look. What do you think?"

"Let's do it!"

"I was thinking, you should apply for a place at the

college. I reckon you'd get into the singing course. You're better than half the kids there even now. Dad gives me a lift most days, or we could get the train in together."

That did make me think. It made me hopeful. Deep down I knew I shouldn't really have left school. These days it seems like you have to go through school, and beyond that, if you want to get anywhere. I'd never planned to leave altogether, just till I sorted myself out, but I hadn't thought of any solution. All I knew was that if I'd stayed at school any longer I would have killed someone, and that someone might have been myself. The college sounded better than a normal school. I liked the idea of being with creative people all day long.

I attacked the blackberries with new vigor. Jessica was a good worker. She seemed to enjoy it, amazingly enough. And having some company did make time pass faster.

Mr. Carruthers arrived just before lunchtime. He brought a whole heap of food: bread rolls, salami, sun-dried tomatoes and capsicums, cheese, mushrooms, plus some cakes. It was a pretty good peace offering, although I did cynically think that if I checked the estate accounts later I'd probably find he'd claimed it under petty cash.

He was in quite a subdued mood. After we'd had a picnic on the lawn beside the old fountain, the exfountain, he asked me if we could have a chat. Jess tactfully went for a walk, and I sat there raising my eyebrows at Mr. Carruthers, waiting for him to make the first move.

"Well, I'm glad to find you in good spirits," he said. "I was worrying all night about you. I actually rang a couple of times but you must have been out."

"Yeah, I went to the McGills' for dinner."

"Winter, I've been looking into the management of the property. It's too early to come to any conclusions, but I must say there seems to be evidence of some improper practice. If that proves to be the case, then I can only apologize for not being aware of it earlier. It is very difficult though, with me being in the city, and only able to come out here every three months. And I've never claimed to be an expert on agriculture. Ralph and Sylvia had excellent references, and from what I saw they were doing everything that could have been expected. But the potential for dishonesty was there, and they may well have succumbed to it."

"So what happens next?"

"I suggest we advertise for a new couple to take over. And I think it would be good if you were involved in the selection process. I feel it's very important that we have a couple you can work with. Quite frankly, if Ralph and Sylvia decide to play it hard, we might have to make a substantial pay-out to them, unless we can prove criminal activity. The estate can't afford any more mistakes like this. We have to get it right next time."

He made it sound like it was my fault that Ralph and Sylvia were crooks.

"OK," I said. "Let's advertise. There's no harm in doing that. But I don't want anyone here for a little bit. I know I'll need someone eventually, but just for a few weeks I want to be on my own. Well, with Jess maybe. She's offered to move into the homestead."

"But what about farming problems? You don't know anything about farming, surely. And Jessica — I can't remember what her father said, but isn't she doing music? That's not necessarily a good recommendation for cattle work."

"I know. But I think Mr. Kennedy, next door, will help."

"Hmm. Well, at least we're agreed on putting the advertisement in, so let's do that for a start. In the meantime I suppose you can always call a consultant, or a vet if there's an urgent problem. Expensive way of doing things though."

Not as expensive as Ralph and Sylvia, I thought.

I was glad to see him go. I stood waving as the big Toyota turned out of the driveway. I was keen to get back to the blackberries.

CHAPTER SIXTEEN

BEFORE I LEFT CANBERRA, DURING the long train journey, and many times since I'd been back, I'd wondered if I'd feel my parents' presence at Warriewood. Would they haunt my footsteps? Would they appear at night? Would they invade my dreams? Maybe they'd be like guardian angels, and warn me if I was in danger. I wondered if they'd be happy at my being there, but for some strange reason I often imagined them as angry, like dark clouds of thunder. I didn't know why they might have been angry.

That first night I spent at the homestead, there was a strong sense of life, and energy, but it wasn't like ghosts. I don't know if there's meant to be a difference between ghosts and spirits, according to the experts, but using the words the way I want to use them, the spirit of my parents was in the homestead but there were no ghosts.

After a couple of weeks I'd stopped thinking about stuff like that much. So it was a shock when I walked toward a paddock I hadn't been in before, and felt a force so strong that it almost winded me. I mean, literally. It was like the air had been punched out of my stomach. Suddenly I was gasping for air, looking around to see if a UFO had landed and was sucking up the atmosphere. I got the most awful sickening feelings. I actually had to retreat. Like, physically.

I walked backwards quite a way, maybe fifty meters, staring at the fence line, thinking: *This is where it happened.* Well, I didn't think it, I knew it. Then it went from being a psychic force to being a memory. Like an old photo, on a wall too long, until the sun shining through the window for years has faded large parts. Now all I could see were shadows and pale patches and a few indistinct images. I strained hard in my mind to see more clearly. They were faces, all faces. Old faces. Two in particular. In my memory they looked about eighty, but I guess to a little kid any adult looks really old. They were staring. They seemed horrible. Staring and shouting and being very, very angry. Then they broke up again, falling apart, crumbling like biscuits in the rain.

The day was bright and sunny but there was no warmth in the air. Autumn was too far gone. But where I stood the ground appeared shadowed, like a darkness was over it. A dark skin seemed to lie across the grass. I backed away further.

Warriewood had always been beautiful to me. As a

little kid I guess I loved it in that accepting way kids have. I don't imagine I stopped to wonder if my life was different from other kids'.

Before I'd worked out how lucky I was, it was all over. I went to Canberra and spent twelve years dreaming about Warriewood, trying to re-create it in my mind. I was like the guy in some movie I saw, cutting bits out of magazines: eyes, eyebrows, a nose, a chin, desperately trying to put together the face of a woman he'd met once and lost. At least with Warriewood I'd had plenty of photos. Ralph and Sylvia, and Mr. Carruthers, had sent me heaps in the first few years, though more recently they'd stopped bothering.

But now it seemed as though Warriewood had turned on me, had shown me another side, dark and threatening. It shook me worse than anything that had happened since I got back. I walked towards the homestead, my arms wrapped around my body, hugging myself, like I did quite often, had always done. I felt that hugs were few and far between in my life. The homestead seemed cold and empty, although it really wasn't that cold a day. But I didn't seem able to find a warm place.

In the end I crawled into bed, after piling every heavy piece of clothing I owned on top of me, and curled up in a little ball under the weight. I fell asleep with my thumb in my mouth.

CHAPTER SEVENTEEN

I TRIED EVERYTHING I COULD think of before I went back to Bannockburn, my Great-aunt Rita's place. I called in at the local paper, the *Christie Courier*, and searched their archives. There was a long article about my mother's death — except it was really about her life. Heaps of details about her riding and shooting trophies, about the Border terriers she'd bred, about her work for Meals on Wheels and the Exley Art Show committee and the Christie Preschool.

She sounded like a bit of a saint. I knew one thing for sure: I'd never live up to her standards.

The *Courier* said she'd died in a shooting accident, but it didn't give any details.

At Jessica's suggestion I tried to track down the cop who'd investigated my mother's death. There must have been a cop. But I got nowhere with that. The Christie police weren't interested. The only thing they did was check the personnel records. They said a Sergeant Bruxton was in charge back then, but no one at the station knew him or had even heard of him.

At Matthew's suggestion I tried the courthouse in

Exley, to see if there were records of a coroner's inquest. They were quite helpful. A bloke with an accent so Scottish that I had trouble understanding it spent nearly half an hour looking through old files. Eventually he found one paragraph about the inquiry: the date, the name of the coroner, my mother's name, and the verdict: death by misadventure.

"What does that mean?" I asked him.

"An accident without concomitant crime or negligence," he said, without batting an eyelid.

"A what?"

I got it on the third go, after Jess persuaded him to say it in Australian, and he drawled it out, taking about five minutes to say "concomitant," which was the word I stuck on.

As I gradually met various neighbors, I asked the ones I liked for any details they knew, but I didn't get any further with them. I know Mr. Kennedy asked a few people too, but they all said the same thing: Ask Mrs. Harrison, ask Mrs. Stone.

Then one day Matthew said to me: "Why don't you go see Dr. Couples?"

"Dr. who?"

"No, that's the name of an old TV show."

"Oh very funny. Who's Dr. Couples?"

"He was the only doctor in Christie. He's retired now, but he's still very fit, does the odd locum when he's needed. He lives in that big brick place on the edge of town, the last house on the right."

I thought this was quite a brilliant suggestion. I wanted to call him straight away, but there was a slight problem when I found he had an unlisted number. Mr. McGill tracked it down for me, and three days later I was ringing the doctor's doorbell, listening to chimes that sounded like a bad orchestra warming up to rehearse elevator music.

After a while I heard soft feet. The door opened to reveal a tall stooped slim man with thinning white hair.

"No need to ask who you are," he said. "Come in."

He had a nice calm voice. I followed him into a big room with one of those gas log fires that seem so real you have to look three times to be sure they are fake. The walls were so covered with family photos you couldn't see much of the brickwork behind them.

Dr. Couples sat at a desk and looked at me in that typical doctor way they all seem to have. Even though he was retired, it was like he had slipped straight into his doctor mode. He even put on that interested, concerned, so-how-can-I-help-you-today face.

"So how can I help you, Winter?" he asked. I nearly cracked up.

He added: "I must say it's nice that you're back here. The last time I saw you was such a terrible occasion, and I felt very much for you."

"That's what I wanted to ask you about," I began. "About my mother dying like that. I didn't know till I came back to Warriewood that she'd died in a shooting accident. And it's been really bugging me. It doesn't seem right. I thought maybe you'd know more about it than anyone."

"What about it doesn't seem right?" he asked.

"Well, the whole thing. It's just too dumb to be true. How can someone with her experience, her knowledge, have an accident like that?"

"People do it all the time," he said, with a tired little smile.

"I guess. It just doesn't match up with the picture I have of her. I imagine the people who get shot accidentally are either pissed — sorry, drunk — or stupid, or not very experienced with guns."

"Not always," Dr. Couples said. He rubbed his eyes with the back of his hand. Suddenly he did look old.

"Was she . . ." I felt the familiar trembling sensation again, as though I could feel myself going white through my whole body, not just the outside but the inside as well. "Was she terribly upset about my father's death?"

"Oh yes. They had a remarkable relationship. The only way I can describe it is to say it was a true love affair. You don't see many in real life, you know. Only in movies or on TV. But they were genuinely devoted to

108

each other. She actually got more upset about Phillip's loss as time went on."

"How depressed was she?"

"That depends on how you use the word 'depressed.' Of course, laymen sometimes use it very differently from the way the medical profession uses it. Phyllis wasn't clinically depressed, in my judgment, but she was feeling deep grief, and great sadness. Entirely natural, but there's no short-term solution to that kind of thing."

"Do you think she was so depressed she . . . she might have given up?"

"Oh no. No. That wasn't Phyllis's way. Not at all. Surely not."

I didn't say any more. I'd worked out just a couple of days earlier, in one of those stupid chains of thought you have while pulling out blackberries, that people often use silence to get other people to talk. I mean, if you ask a question, someone gives an answer; but if you don't say any more, they eventually always add something. I suppose I noticed it while listening to the radio. I often had it on when I was doing blackberries, and I think I'd been listening to a programme on Triple J where the interviewer had done exactly that.

So now I thought I'd see if it worked for me.

Sure enough, to my delight, after a minute Dr. Couples kept talking. "It was a terrible tragedy, coming so soon after your father's death. Just terrible.

Everyone was devastated. I admit though, I did wonder if she had been less attentive because of your father's death. I can imagine that maybe she wasn't concentrating the way she normally would."

"But could it have been something more than that?" I asked, leaning forward, watching him anxiously. "Do you think she was depressed enough . . . to do that?"

I expected him to look shocked, but maybe you can't shock doctors.

"I got there before the ambulance, you know. The Christie ambulance was miles away, over near Exley I think. We'd been agitating for years to get a second ambulance but the Minister showed no interest at all. We've got three now of course. Well, when I arrived — it would have been around four o'clock in the afternoon — she was lying beside the fence. Mrs. Harrison was there. She'd tried some first aid, but to no effect. When she realized Phyllis was dead, she and the housekeeper lifted her onto the back of the pickup truck and put a handkerchief over her face."

"I thought you weren't meant to do that," I said. "I thought you were supposed to leave everything alone, so the police could investigate."

"Well, that's true, of course, but in the heat of the moment people frequently do things they're not meant to."

"I guess."

"But as for what you're suggesting, well, there was no evidence one way or the other. I didn't think it necessary to conduct a thorough examination. It all seemed clear enough. I checked for vital signs, but she had been killed instantly. I suppose, looking back, and being as honest as you can be only after you've retired, I would say the last thing I wanted to do was to play the TV super-medic and comb through the grass for clues. I've given my life to the people of this district. They're very important to me. I would never cause them unnecessary grief."

I wondered if he was telling me in a roundabout way that he'd thought at the time she might have committed suicide, but he had deliberately closed his mind to the possibility.

"Was I actually there?" I asked.

"No, apparently you were at the homestead with Mrs. Stone. I didn't see you at all. I asked if I should, if you were upset or distressed, but Mrs. Harrison assured me you were all right, that you didn't know yet, and she'd explain it to you gently. I think she'd called Mrs. Stone as soon as it happened, but when they realized nothing could be done, Mrs. Stone went back to the house to took after you."

I tried my silence tactic again, but this time it didn't work. Maybe he had told me everything he knew. After a minute of us sitting looking at each other I realized there wasn't much more I could ask.

I got up.

"Thanks a lot for seeing me," I said. "And for telling me all that."

"It's a pleasure to see you back at Warriewood," he said. "And grown into such a fine young woman. Let me know if I can help you in any way."

He said it without much meaning though, like he was tired of helping people. He'd had enough.

CHAPTER EIGHTEEN

I WAS AT A BARBECUE WITH Matthew Kennedy, trying to work out something I could dislike about him. I mean, I'm not a complete jerk, I don't go around trying to find horrible things about people, but I was a bit worried by how perfect he seemed.

The barbecue was at Matthew's mum's. She lived in a little house surrounded by a high hedge, about ten k's from Warriewood. I didn't know anyone there — I'd gone with Matthew, but just, you know, definitely not a date — and the first thing I realized was that everyone knew me.

Most of them were a lot older than Matthew and me. They were friends of Mrs. Kennedy, but there were two boys about our age, and a girl called Astrid, who lived next door. It was a hot day, totally wrong for autumn, and the barbecue was around the pool, although no one was tempted to go in. We hung around one end of the pool while the adults stayed up the other end. Mostly. It was kind of obvious the adults were checking me out. They all found reasons to drop in and have a chat, and for every one question aimed at the others I got ten.

I didn't say much though. I don't know whether they thought I was rude, but I don't like feeling I'm on display, in a zoo, even an open-range one.

One of the boys, a guy named Tim Glass, seemed like fun, so I talked to him a fair bit. We were at one of those little tables with an umbrella over it. Matt sat on the edge of the pool stirring the water with a walking stick and chatting up Astrid. Tim was heavily into *Lord of the Rings*, which I'd read a couple of years back, and *The Hitchhiker's Guide to the Galaxy*, which I'd never read, and Stephen King, who I'm quite into. He had just finished *The Green Mile*, a book I'd bought in Canberra but still hadn't read. So we talked about books for a while, then Canberra.

"We went to Canberra for our grade-six excursion," he said.

"Yeah? You and every other kid in Australia. Let me guess, Parliament House, the War Memorial, the art gallery, and that science place?"

"That's about right. We met the Prime Minister, I remember that. If you can call it meeting. He stopped for four seconds, got his photo taken, and hurried off to do something more important."

"He'd probably figured that by the time you were old enough to vote, he would have retired."

It was a relief that we weren't talking about Warriewood or my parents.

"The main thing I remember about that trip was

the teachers threatening to send us home, when we got caught on the roof of the girls' showers."

"You little perv. They should have sent you home."

"Bit hard, isn't it? Like, how do they send you home from Canberra?"

"Mmm, it is a long walk."

He went into a long spiel about a school trip to Nouméa they'd done last year, and how he'd nearly been sent home from that too, because they suspected him of smoking dope, but they couldn't prove it.

I suddenly started getting a bit sick of him. He reminded me of a comic strip I'd seen once where a guy is talking to a girl and he's saying "I, I, I, I, I . . ." for about ten minutes, then she says "I" once and he promptly falls asleep on the table.

I poured him another drink and glanced across at Matthew. He was flicking water with the stick and listening to Astrid. I'd never seen him listen to someone for so long before. It was the opposite to the guy in the comic strip. Beside me Tim was saying, "So do you want to?"

I realized I'd completely missed something. From the look on his face it seemed like it was important. He was leaning closer. I started to get a pretty good idea of what he'd said.

"Uh, sorry?" I asked, embarrassed that I hadn't even heard.

"Forget it," he said, leaning back again. "I can see who you belong to."

"Belong to?" I said, swinging around so I was side-on to him. "Belong to?"

He stood up and slouched away, to the other end of the pool. I was furious. I decided I'd been completely wrong about him being a nice guy. I slumped in my chair, folded my arms, crossed my feet at the ankles and thought, *Yes, I really do have a special way with guys.*

Matthew left Astrid and came towards me, like he was on his way into the house. He stopped and looked down at me. Squinting into the sun, I was impressed by how tall he was.

"Do you want anything?" he asked. "I'm just getting some block-out for Astrid."

"Yeah, I wouldn't mind a squirt of it too," I said, thinking that I wouldn't mind Matthew rubbing some into me. "I'll give you a hand."

Inside the house everything was neat and pretty. A bit too pretty I thought, but I remembered my manners and didn't say so. I watched from the bathroom door as Matthew rummaged through the cupboard.

"So you like Tim, huh?" he asked, pulling out a couple of tubes, but not looking at me.

I was about to say "No thanks," but then thought better of it and said, "Yeah, he's pretty cute."

The back of Matthew's neck did seem to go a little red. Or was I imagining that?

When he didn't say anything, I added: "Astrid seems nice."

"Yeah," he said, standing up. "Yeah, I've known Astrid since we jumped off the garage roof together, about twelve years ago. Kind of brings you closer to someone, doing that."

"Why did you jump off the garage roof?"

"We'd been watching *Mary Poppins*, so we armed ourselves with umbrellas and took off, holding hands."

He was standing very close to me now, waiting to get out of the bathroom, except I was in his way.

"Did you hurt yourselves? Or is that a dumb question?"

He held his left arm up to my face. A long white scar ran along the inside of it, nearly all the way from his wrist to his shoulder.

"Wow. That's some scar."

"You want to kiss it better?" He moved his arm a little closer, and he leaned towards me, like it was really his mouth that wanted kissing better.

For a moment I hesitated. I was tempted. I sure was. Then I shook my head slowly.

"I've got a few things to sort out."

I fled outside, at a dignified fast walk.

That's why I thought I'd better find some stuff to not like about Matthew. If I didn't I might do something really dumb, like fall in love with him.

CHAPTER NINETEEN

AND SO THE TIME CAME WHEN I was forced to face the fact that my last hope was Great-aunt Rita at Bannockburn. Great-aunt Rita and Mrs. Stone, the housekeeper. I had put the moment off as long as I could. I was so nervous of meeting her that I even wondered if there was something from the past preying on my mind. Some unhappy memory of her, some cruelty from my childhood, that lay beneath the surface, like a giant sleeping squid.

Jess offered to come with me, but I refused. With my hand pressed to my heart, as she threw cushions at me, I said: "There are some things a girl has to do on her own, before she can call herself a man."

Jessica just threw more cushions.

The day of my audition for the College of the Arts was the day I decided to go to Bannockburn. I thought I might as well make it the day from hell and be done with it. I was so nervous about the audition, because it had been more than two months since my last lesson with Mrs. Scanelli. I had a couple of warm-up lessons with a nice old man in Christie, who had been in some operas with Joan Sutherland. His name was Gregory O'Mara. He was a very funny guy, the most openly gay man I'd ever met. He spent more time talking about his boyfriends than teaching me singing, but he knew his stuff, and I thought if I didn't get into the college I might see if I could do regular lessons with him.

The audition was at ten o'clock in the morning, which isn't a good time for anyone's voice, especially mine. I thought they should have known that, and not had any early morning auditions, but I don't know, maybe they made allowances. I did a piece of my choice, "Unforgettable," and a compulsory one, a Bach song called "Bist du bei mir," and the usual scales and stuff. I messed up a bit of the middle section of the Bach, and got one of the scales wrong, but otherwise it seemed to go OK.

The two teachers were like the good-cop, bad-cop: one was all sweet and nice and smiling and the other sat there frowning like she thought the college already had enough students and I should go back to Christie before I totally destroyed their reputation and made them the laughingstock of the music world.

It was a relief to get outside, back into the fresh air. Jess had classes so I had to go off and get the train to Christie on my own. I deliberately didn't let myself think about Great-aunt Rita because I was still recovering from the audition. In fact, every time I pictured

119

going up that awful big driveway, nasty scary thoughts started to sneak into my mind. So I told myself: You don't have to go there, you can just go straight home.

I figured if I kept saying that I could put off any decision until I was standing in front of the gates of Bannockburn.

Feeling extravagant, and too tired to get the bus, I caught the Christie taxi from the station. There are only a couple of taxis in Christie, but I hadn't seen this driver before. It was a pretty quiet trip, after he made a comment in the first few minutes about Vietnamese drivers. "Don't know how those bloody slopies get their licenses" were his actual words.

What a prick, I thought, too tired to argue with him, or to point out where he rated on the scale of losers. Some days you just can't be bothered. I paid him off at the entrance to Bannockburn and even gave him a tip, of nearly two bucks, which shows how tired and not in the mood I was.

I waited till he'd done his U-turn and gone, then I walked through the gates again.

The driveway seemed longer than ever. The house seemed bigger, and the whole place colder. It felt like no one young had been in there for a hundred years. Forgetting the promise I'd made, the let-off I'd offered myself when I was leaving the college, I walked up the driveway, my feet crunching on the white gravel. With that kind of gravel I got a strong impression I was going nowhere. Somehow it slowed me down, rolling as I walked in it, so I seemed to be slipping backwards.

Even the front door was impressive. Big dark red wood, with a solid brass knocker. I cowered in the shadow of the door for a minute, but I knew that having come this far, if I didn't go through with it I'd never return. Quickly, before I could change my mind, I gave a sharp rat-a-tat-tat with the knocker.

God, it was the loudest noise I'd ever heard. It echoed through the house like a thunderclap. I could hear it dying slowly as it went from room to room. I began to seriously doubt whether anyone lived here at all. Maybe the old lady had died. Maybe she'd moved to Majorca. Maybe she was down in the old grannies' home. Was there a home for great-aunts?

It seemed like half an hour before anything happened. Lucky it did. I knew I wasn't game to give the knocker a second go. It was all or nothing. But eventually I heard slow footsteps crossing an uncovered floor. It seemed another ten minutes before the door actually opened. It was hard to see the woman's face, because it was so dark. I peered in, wondering if I would recognize her. She stared back. I didn't recognize her, but I knew she'd recognized me.

"Winter?"

"Yes. Are you . . . ?"

"No, I'm not her. I'm the housekeeper."

"Mrs. Stone?"

"Yes. Fancy you remembering."

"I didn't really. But a few people have told me your name, and that you live here."

There was a pause, neither of us knowing what to say.

"Do you want me to ask if she'll see you?"

"Uh, yes please."

I was a bit disconcerted by the "if she'll see you." Why wouldn't she see me? I was her great-niece, and I planned on trying hard to be a really great great-niece. How many relatives did she have? Surely not so many that she could afford to be choosy.

I had lost all sense of the relativity of time, but I know I waited a lot longer for Mrs. Stone to return from the trip upstairs than I had for her to open the door. I reckon it could have been fifteen minutes. By then I was sitting on the steps outside, leaning against a little brick wall. When I heard her coming I jumped up, embarrassed to have her catch me being so casual. This didn't seem like a casual house.

Something, maybe the way she dragged her feet, told me that Mrs. Stone had failed. When she did get back to the door she said simply: "She won't see you."

"She won't see me," I repeated, stupidly.

"She's not very well."

But the way she said that, like it was just a token excuse, made it obvious that health wasn't the big issue here.

I felt wounded, like a bird shot in the breast. I felt the arrow penetrate my skin and touch my heart.

"Oh," I said, pushing my hair away from my eyes. I'd never seriously imagined this would happen, and now it had I didn't know how to deal with it. My eyes were stinging.

Somehow though I couldn't bring myself to turn away and walk down that long lonely driveway. I started getting angry that I'd come so far, and for nothing.

I didn't think it through, but in my mind was something like: She should see me, she can't have many relatives, she should be especially nice to the few she's got. And then: I don't have many relatives. I need the ones I've got. I can't afford to lose any more.

Like a three-year-old throwing a tantrum, I said to Mrs. Stone: "I'm not going. I'll stay here until she sees me."

Mrs. Stone lived up to her name. Without a flicker of expression she said, "It's no good. I'm sorry. Once she makes up her mind she never changes it."

Suddenly the casual comment I'd made became a definite commitment. I sat on the doorstep, in a position that made it impossible for her to close the door, and said, "I'll stay here for as long as it takes."

Now she was flustered. She changed from being solid and steady and cool, to nervous and uncertain.

"Winter, please, don't be unreasonable about this.

Mrs. Harrison isn't going to see you today. Maybe another day. Why don't you write her a letter? I'll make sure she gets it."

I folded my arms, set my mouth in a line about as thin and straight as the slot on an ATM machine, and said, "This is a sit-in. I'll stay here for a week if I have to."

"My God," she said. "You're as stubborn as she is."

But there was a note of something — excitement even? — in her voice. I guess if nothing much had happened in this house for a long time, a sit-in would count as reasonably spectacular.

She hurried away, her heels clicking on the parquet floor.

I sat there and gazed around. The front door opened into a room where you could have parked a couple of semi-trailers. Not that Great-aunt Rita would be heavily into semi-trailers. It was a beautiful room. It was just an entrance hall, but on the left-hand side was a huge marble fireplace, which looked like it had never been used, and on the right-hand side a statue of a naked goddess, with a panther or something beside her. There was one of those things on the ceiling, like a big round flower, made of plaster I think, and painted in brown and yellow and blue. It must have taken about three weeks just to paint it. Great-aunt Rita obviously had a heap of money. Maybe she was worried I wanted to get some off her. But I didn't care about that. I had enough of my own, despite the huge amount Mr. Carruthers took from me every year in management fees.

At the end of the entrance hall was a staircase that looked like marble too. It was hard to tell, because the light down that end was dim, but I figured there wouldn't be anything fake in this house. If it looked like marble it probably was marble. Two curved handrails, one on each side, made the whole thing seem graceful and female.

Mrs. Stone had gone up those stairs, so Great-aunt Rita was on the top floor somewhere. I considered for a moment whether I should just charge up and find her, but that didn't seem like a good idea. I had the feeling that Great-aunt Rita would value good manners, and I was already so far over the line on that one that I thought I'd better not go any further.

I sat gazing at the marble staircase, waiting for Mrs. Stone to return.

She didn't.

It wasn't very comfortable on the floor, but I was determined not to move. I just kept shifting my position every time my bum got numb.

On the wall on the left-hand side, above the fireplace, was a painting of a woman who was unmistakably my mother. Dressed in old farm clothes, holding a dog that looked like a Border terrier, she stared out at me with a direct and clear gaze. I wondered if I'd be as strong as I was now if she hadn't died. She was so obviously a powerful personality, and I knew from watching my school friends that sometimes a mother like that can overrun you. I'd seen quite a few families with powerful parents and passive kids. Like, there was only so much room in the family, and the parents took most of it.

Maybe my mother, by dying, had given me the space to become strong.

I wasn't sure whether what I was doing now was strong or pathetic. What could they do? Throw me out? I knew I was physically stronger than Mrs. Stone, and she'd know it too. And Mrs. Harrison didn't sound like she was in any shape to manhandle me. Get someone else to throw me out? The police? I was willing to bet Mrs. Harrison wouldn't bring shame on the family name, and embarrassment on herself, by doing that. Imagine if word went round the district — "refused to see her niece . . . called the police . . . had her thrown out of the house . . . wouldn't give her the time of day . . . after twelve years!" Even if Mrs. Harrison was a recluse, I didn't think she'd risk her reputation to that extent.

So maybe she'd starve me out. The whole thing could become a big joke. Seriously, what would happen if three days later I was still camped on the doorstep? What would I do for food and water? And, most importantly, how would I go to the toilet?

As soon as I thought of that I immediately felt the urge to go. It's so annoying how that happens. I tried to drive the idea out of my head and think of something else. The word "camped' had reminded me of something. Oh yes. The Aboriginal Tent Embassy, in Canberra. I'd seen it often enough. Maybe I could copy them. If I got to the point where I was desperate for food and water, I would go home, get a good supply, come back with a tent, and literally camp on Great-aunt Rita's front lawn. That'd give her something to think about. It didn't solve the toilet problem, but it was a nice idea.

After twenty minutes, when there was still no sign of Mrs. Stone, I sneaked out to the front garden and peed behind a box hedge, then scuttled back, hoping that she hadn't noticed me missing. I was worried she might have run downstairs the moment my back was turned and slammed the door.

But nothing had changed.

Three hours later there still wasn't much change. Twice I'd seen Mrs. Stone come halfway down the stairs, peer at me, then go back up — to report, I suppose.

I could imagine the conversation:

"She's still there."

"All right, unchain the dogs."

A couple of times I heard footsteps on the floor above, and once I thought I heard voices, but in a big house like that it's hard to work out all the sounds.

I was almost enjoying myself, in a weird kind of way. I think never in my life have I felt so in the right. I really thought I was justified in being there, that my great-aunt had to see me. She simply couldn't turn me away.

My main short-term concern was whether Jess would get home and start to worry about me. It would soon be dark outside, and although Jess and I were pretty casual about each other's movements, she might worry, especially knowing I'd had the big audition that morning.

I amused myself by imagining how it would go if I finally did get to meet Great-aunt Rita.

"Lovely house," I would say. "I do so admire your roses. Wonderful how you keep them flowering at this time of year."

"Well, my dear, of course it's the three gardeners who do the actual work. Along with their assistants. And apprentices. And the groundsmen. But it's so hard to find good help these days."

"Oh I know. Isn't it just awful?"

Or would she come down the staircase waving a walking stick like a wand and shouting curses:

"You stubborn pig-headed little fool! How dare

128

you invade my house! Get out! You're as bad as your rotten no-good mother. No wonder she killed herself."

I was almost disappointed when one of these day-dreams was interrupted by Mrs. Stone.

"Winter," she said, coming towards me and look-ing genuinely distressed. "You really must go. Mrs. Harrison is becoming most upset."

"Not as upset as I am," I said, without getting up.

"I don't understand," she said. "What is it you want?"

"I want to see my great-aunt," I said. "Is that so un-usual? What's wrong with that?"

"But she . . . I'm sure you can understand she has very strong feelings . . . about what happened. She still has them. She doesn't want to be reminded . . ." After a pause she added: "She's an old woman. Why can't you leave her in peace?"

"I won't. I can't. I have to see her. And if she won't see me now I'll go home and get a tent and come back and camp on the front lawn for however long it takes. Months if I have to."

With a shake of her head Mrs. Stone turned away. As she re-crossed the parquet, I yelled after her, "And I'll take that portrait of my mother with me."

"That's not your mother," a voice said. "It's me."

I looked up. Standing on the first landing was an old lady dressed in a heavy gold-and-white dressing

129

gown. She looked magnificent, like a Chinese empress or something. In her hand was a walking stick, so my daydream was right in that detail.

The walking stick made her look fierce. I half expected her to throw it at me. I bet she wouldn't have missed, either.

I stood, and stared at her. She stared back. She didn't look fierce really, just strong. She could have stared at me all day without blinking or looking away. She was like a wedge-tailed eagle.

"You've got what you came for," she said. "You've seen me. Now you can go."

But we both knew I wouldn't be doing that.

"That's not what I came for," I said.

"What then?"

"I want to ask you a question."

I'd surprised her. At the foot of the stairs Mrs. Stone turned towards me, an expression on her face that I couldn't identify from the quick glance I gave her. Mrs. Harrison came slowly down the staircase, looking occasionally at where she should put her feet, but most of the time still staring hard at me.

She got to the bottom of the stairs and walked towards me. Her steps sounded firm and steady on the floor, despite the walking stick. She stopped when she was two meters away.

"What is it you want to know?" she asked.

"How did my mother die?"

130

I heard a gasp from behind her. Mrs. Stone's footsteps came quickly across the floor towards me too, but they sounded light and kind of temporary compared to Mrs. Harrison's.

I didn't look at Mrs. Stone.

"Do you mean to tell me you really don't know? You don't remember?"

"No."

I shook my head. I was getting scared. Something was wrong.

Mrs. Stone's face appeared beside Mrs. Harrison's. Suddenly they were both there, staring at me. Two old faces, screwed up with horror. Two faces that seemed to be cracking, falling apart, disintegrating, as they stared into what I had done. Yes, me, Winter De Salis.

And with a great terrible rush of discovery I found I did know. And realized I had always known. I gave a cry, a terrible cry, and ran out of the house with my hands over my eyes. I didn't want to look anymore, didn't want to see the terrible sight. I ran and ran and ran, down the long tormenting white drive of my memory, down the long black bitumen road of terror, and at last, as I reached Warriewood, between the stone gateposts of my childhood.

CHAPTER TWENTY

"**A**RE YOU ALL RIGHT NOW?" Jessica asked.

I nodded.

"You were hysterical. I've never seen anyone so upset. At first I thought you must have done the worst audition in the history of the college."

I grinned and nodded and hiccupped.

"I think it went OK," I said.

"Do you want another coffee?"

"No. Is there any more of that carrot cake?"

"That sounds promising. You must be getting better."

"I haven't eaten anything much since last night. Too nervous."

"Well, my carrot cake'll either fill you or kill you."

When she came back with the cake she said, "God I'm sorry about that last crack. I can't believe I was so insensitive. I've been trying to find a knife to slash my wrists, but there's not much in the kitchen."

"What last crack?" I searched in my memory then worked out what she'd said.

"Oh. Oh yes. I guess that was a poor choice of words."

She watched as I ate, then said, "Will you keep living here?"

"I don't know. At first, as I was coming up the drive, I was thinking: *I just want to pack my bags and get out.* But I don't know. I do love Warriewood. It's the only place that feels like home. And I've always felt I belong here. I don't know if places really can have memories."

"It's so amazing. I can hardly believe it. How old were you?"

"Um, four."

"Amazing. Do you really think a four-year-old could do that?"

"I guess."

There was a knock on the front door. We hadn't even heard a car. But a few moments later Jessica returned with someone unexpected.

Mrs. Stone.

"Your aunt sent me to see if you were all right," she said.

"Yes, thanks. I'm OK."

"Can I get you a cup of tea?" Jessica asked.

After a moment she said, "Thank you, perhaps I will."

"Winter, you still don't want another coffee?"

"No, I'm fine."

When Jess had gone off to the kitchen, Mrs. Stone said to me: "This is the first time I've been here since it happened really. A week after the funeral I took the job with Mrs. Harrison."

"I'm sorry it looks so shabby," I said. "The renovations are about to start. This room'll have a soft lemony sort of ceiling, and the same down to the dado, then quite a dark yellow for the rest. And the floors'll be polished."

"I'm sure you'll do a wonderful job."

There was a bit of silence, then I said, "I'm sorry, but I told Jess. I imagine you and my aunt don't want anyone to know. I mean, it could get you in trouble, couldn't it? Interfering with evidence or something."

It was like I'd unblocked a valve then, because she started talking. For the first time in twelve years probably.

"I think it is better to keep it quiet still. Although perhaps no one would care much anymore. It's such a long time ago. The policeman, Detective Sergeant Bruxton his name was, we'd known him for a long time. Perhaps he did wonder if there was something else . . . but not what . . . what actually happened. He dropped a couple of hints, as though he thought she might have ended her own life, I mean deliberately, and we'd fixed it to make it look like an accident. If he suspected anything he suspected that."

134

"That's what I thought had happened," I said, as Jessica came back into the room, with a tea for Mrs. Stone and a coffee for herself. Somehow she'd found a couple of Wagon Wheels and cut them into little shapes and arranged them on a plate. I guess I'd just eaten the last slice of carrot cake. It didn't look as elegant as the afternoon teas that I imagine Mrs. Stone would serve up to Great-aunt Rita, or Great-aunt Rita's friends, if she had any.

But I'm a Wagon Wheel addict, so I grabbed a piece, and Mrs. Stone took one without even noticing what she was doing. I think she was too engrossed in her story.

She looked shocked by my reference to suicide though. "Phyllis take her own life? Good heavens no. That's the last thing Phyllis would have done. Phyllis was a fighter. Nothing would have stopped . . ."

Then she looked embarrassed as she realized that something had stopped Phyllis. Something as powerful as a bullet.

"But people told me she got more and more depressed after my father died," I said, switching the subject, giving her a chance to get back on track.

The last thing I wanted was for her to stop talking. I was listening avidly to every word. This was my history. The gap in my life was slowly being filled, brick by brick, word by word.

"Yes, I think that's true," Mrs. Stone said. "But

135

they had been so deeply in love. Phyllis attracted love. People who'd only met her once or twice spoke of her as though they loved her, as though she were their best friend. Mrs. Harrison was utterly devoted to her. She thought of Phyllis as the daughter she'd never had. That's why she was so devastated . . . that's why she didn't want to see you. Do you know, she's never spoken of Phyllis, or the . . . the day of the accident, from that moment on?"

"How did it actually happen?" I asked, as gently as I could.

This was the critical moment. If I could get her to tell me this bit, I thought I might be satisfied.

She hesitated, looking at Jessica.

"Uh, is this where I leave?" Jess asked, getting up.

"No it's fine," I said, too quickly, as I realized when I saw Mrs. Stone hesitate again.

One thing about Jess, she was perceptive. She picked up on little clues. Just like her father. Or else she wouldn't have moved in the first place.

"I'll go," she said. "Would you like another cup of tea?"

"No, no thanks, that was very nice."

Jessica did her exit. I wanted her to stay, for moral support, but I don't think Mrs. Stone would have talked freely with anyone else there.

Even with Jess out of the room, Mrs. Stone had trouble getting started. I tried a few prompts.

"So how did it happen?" I said again.

Her head dropped and I thought I saw a little tear fall onto her knee.

"Was she going shooting? Was it over by that paddock with the mulberry trees?"

She nodded, and sniffed. "So you do remember?" she said.

"No, I don't. But I got the weirdest vibes when I was in that paddock. After that I was sure it must have been the place where she died. I don't know if it's memory or what."

"That was her rifle range," she said. "It wasn't a long one, but she liked it because you get such variable wind patterns in that paddock, and she thought it was good for training. Every day the conditions were different."

"So was she practicing that day?" I asked. "Did she take me with her?"

"You were so young," she said. "No one had the slightest idea you could operate a firearm. No one. Phyllis had never taught you. You were just too intelligent for your own good. You must have only seen her operate the safety a couple of times. She had just started training for the national titles, and Mrs. Harrison and I took you over to the paddock, for a little walk, and to see your mummy. It was all so quick. We got there, and Phyllis had two or three guns standing against the back of the truck as well as the one she was using. You picked one of them up — you could barely hold it — and before anyone registered what you were doing, you slid the action forward and fired. I've got an idea you even said 'bang bang' as you pulled the trigger. I thought I saw your mouth forming the words."

She started shaking. "It was just a game to you. Phyllis fell without a word. We tried to stop the bleeding, we tried to revive her, but there was never a chance. She died instantly. When we finally realized there was nothing to be done we just looked at each other. Mrs. Harrison took charge. She didn't have to say anything but I knew what she was thinking. If the press got hold of it, of you, they'd have had a field day. Your aunt, I mean your great-aunt, hated anything like that. She took the gun and put it on the ground behind the pickup truck, as though it had fallen. Then she got the dog and locked him in the cab of the truck. It wasn't easy — the dog was very distressed. He knew something was wrong. But your aunt is such a forceful lady. She lifted the dog and more or less threw him in there. Then she told me to take you to the homestead, here, and call the police, and the doctor. "Don't bring Winter back with you," she said. "You stay in the homestead with her. Just point the police and Dr. Couples in the right direction when they come. Then leave the rest to me."

"'Yes, all right,' I said. She's so clever, I knew I

could trust her to work it out, to fix everything. Sergeant Bruxton did come to the house to talk to me, but I just said I hadn't been there, hadn't seen anything. And like I said, he accepted that. He didn't even ask whether you'd been there, just assumed you hadn't."

"And you never told anyone?"

"I never did," she said. "I have an idea Mrs. Harrison told those people you went to live with, in Canberra, Phyllis's half sister."

"Thank you for telling me now," I said. "And thanks for coming here, to see if I was OK."

"It's nice to see you home at last," she said. "I hear you're doing a fine job, bringing the old place to life again. I hope you're back for good. I'm sure Mrs. Harrison will want to see you, but maybe not for a few days. She was very distressed after you left."

"I'd like to see her again," I said. "I think we might have a bit in common."

CHAPTER TWENTY-ONE

I T WASN'T EASY TO RETURN TO
the graves. The first time I'd gone I'd never thought
that my mother was there because of me.

I'd planned for my second visit that I'd come with
flowers and gardening tools, to make it beautiful. But I
came empty-handed.

I'm not sure what I wanted or expected. Maybe I
was looking for forgiveness. But I don't really think so.
Daughters kill their mothers in all kinds of ways. If not
when they're giving birth, then later. Some of my
friends in Canberra were killing their mothers slowly,
one day at a time, death by a million cuts.

What I had done was weird, one of the freakish
things that happen in life, like an iceberg scraping
along the side of a ship and cutting it open as if it was
made of aluminium. I knew I couldn't be blamed for
what happened when I was four years old.

But I did wonder whether some strange force was
at work that day. How innocent was I when I pulled
the trigger? Surely even at four I had some understanding of what a gun meant, and what it could do.
Was I angry at my mother that afternoon? Had I been

angry at her for some time? Maybe for six months. Maybe for always.

I sat by the grave, picking at the burrs that had started to cover it again. I could never make my peace with my mother now. I could not ask for her understanding. I had to trust to her heart, her spirit. I thought about *Seven Little Australians*, where Judy lies in the hut, shaking with fear to know she's dying at the age of thirteen, and Meg tells her, "You won't be lonely," because their mother, who died four years earlier, would be waiting for her.

Would my mother be waiting for me sometime down the road? Would she have a speech prepared? I had cost her maybe forty years. She was entitled to be angry. God, I would be.

Or would she be pleased, that we were together again?

I pulled at one weed and realized too late that it was a stinging nettle. Wow, did it sting. My fingers went red and hard and hot and swollen. I sat there sucking them, feeling this was a bad omen. Then suddenly it struck me as funny. I'd shot my mother and this was her revenge? To sting my hand for a couple of hours?

I started laughing. People had told me about my mother's sense of humor. Well, the hell with it. I wasn't going to be beaten that easily. I ignored my burning fingers and began weeding the graves.

CHAPTER TWENTY-TWO

S OMEHOW BLOODY MATTHEW
Kennedy got me brushing his horses for him. I
don't know how it happened. But there we were in the
stables, doing alternate stalls, giving each horse a thorough grooming, and talking through the walls, even
though we couldn't see each other.

I was brushing a big black colt named Derek, giving his flanks long firm strokes, watching the muscles
twitch under the steady stroking. I was beginning to
like horses a lot more. I liked the feel of their coats: not
soft or fluffy, not smooth, coarse but flowing, alive
with power.

It was hard work though. I could feel a patch of
sweat in each armpit, and I had to keep stopping and
wiping the hair out of my eyes.

"So what did she talk about?" Matthew asked.

"Family history. I think she wants to tell me all the
stories before she dies. I think she sees me as the
keeper of the stories."

We were talking about my first afternoon tea with
Great-aunt Rita, the day before.

"She's got quite a reputation," Matthew said.

"I can believe it."

"Dad says she looks like you."

"What?" I was so startled I dropped the brush. "Thanks a lot. We're only about seventy years apart."

I went to pick up the brush, then saw his laughing face appear around the side of the stall.

"You're pathetic, Matthew Kennedy. You expect me to do your stable work for free, then you insult me."

I couldn't think of anything cleverer to say. He had me right off balance. I don't know why, nothing to do with comparing me to Great-aunt Rita, just the way I was steamed up from doing the horses, and hot, and still not knowing what kind of relationship I had with Matthew.

I was down on my hands and knees, looking for the brush. Matthew came around the other side of the horse and picked up the brush, which had gone further than I thought. He stayed down at ground level and passed the brush to me under the big colt's legs. But when I went to take it he didn't let go of my hand.

We held hands for a couple of minutes, looking at each other, right in the eyes. We were both very serious. Somehow it wasn't the moment for jokes.

After a while I said softly: "Lots of horses here to be brushed."

"That's right."

But he didn't let go of my hand. Derek, the colt, tossed his head and moved his feet uneasily. It was a kind of weird situation, the two of us under the bridge of the big horse. Maybe I should have been nervous, but I wasn't. We shuffled a little closer together, in the straw. I closed my eyes as our lips met. It was my first kiss, and I hadn't imagined it being like this, but what the hell, I'd never read the script of my life.

Matthew's lips felt dry at first, but then they got more moist, and somehow the more moist they became, the nicer they felt.

I know the kiss lasted a long time. In the end Derek got too restless and we had to move. Maybe he was jealous. We sat outside, on the sand, our backs against the stall door, holding hands and kissing and hardly saying a word. The horses got the sloppiest grooming of all time.

CHAPTER TWENTY-THREE

THE FIRST NIGHT OF MY RETURN to Warriewood I helped Ralph set up my bed in the blue bedroom I'd slept in as a child. I'd never thought that I could move into the bedroom my parents occupied all those years ago. But gradually, as the painters and floor-polishers and electricians and furniture removalists and tilers and all the others came and worked and went, I changed my mind. In the middle of telling them the color for the veranda and how I wanted the curtains and where the vents for the heating system should be and where to put the bookcase, I realized that it was time to move into the main bedroom. I couldn't stay in the small bedroom anymore. It wasn't right. I was the owner of Warriewood now, not a four-year-old.

Whether I wanted to admit it or not, I was in charge.

And so into the main bedroom went a four-poster bed with painted panels at the top and the end, a big jarrah chest of drawers, a cedar wardrobe, a round cedar table, and wallpaper with bluish-green flowers on the lightest yellow background. Because it was looking so adult, and because I'm still a teenager, I put up some posters of Winsome Lloyd, who's my idea of a beautiful chick, and of a Chinese actor called Jordan Chan, and of a band called Zaiko Langa Langa, who no one's ever heard of, but I saw them at Womad. It's not exactly a decorator's idea of what should go with cedar and jarrah furniture, but it works for me.

I moved in on September the first. It's a good room. I like lying there in the mornings, when I first wake up, looking at the walls and the curtains and the furniture. Sometimes I think I should have a little shrine on top of the chest of drawers, like the ones on the side of the road: a bunch of flowers and a card, a toy horse maybe. I only think that because I feel a bit guilty that there's not more signs of my parents in the house, especially in the bedroom. But I know I don't need a shrine to remember them. The main thing for me is to think about their lives, instead of concentrating on the way my mother died. I'm a strong person and somehow I've found the strength to get used to the idea that I pulled that trigger. Get used to the idea but not get destroyed by it. That's what I've had to do, and I've done it. If I'd failed, the bullet would have claimed more than one victim.

Next week, just for a laugh, Jess and I are having a formal dinner party, with ten guests. We're making the guys wear dinner jackets and the girls long dresses. It's a bit of a joke, but it'll be fun. I'm asking Matthew

Kennedy, and Jess has got her man coming all the way from Orange Ag., and there're four friends of Jess's from Christie and four of our friends from school.

I can't wait. Jess is calling it a housewarming, but that's not what I call it. Privately, to myself, I call it a resurrection.

About the Author

JOHN MARSDEN is the author of many acclaimed international best sellers, including *Letters from the Inside* and *A Killing Frost*. He has won numerous awards, including the Christopher Medal and Australia's Children's Book of the Year Award. His novel *Tomorrow When the War Began* was named an ALA Best Book of the last half-century. He lives in Australia.

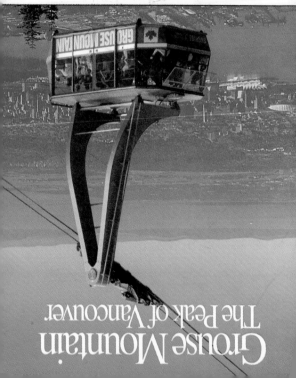

Grouse Mountain
The Peak of Vancouver

Get to the PO**I**NT

The best of teen literature from award-winning authors

Check out these Point books.

☐ 0-590-48141-X	**Make Lemonade,** Virginia Euwer Wolff	$5.99 US
☐ 0-590-40943-3	**Fallen Angels,** Walter Dean Myers	$5.99 US
☐ 0-590-31990-6	**When She Was Good,** Norma Fox Mazer	$5.99 US
☐ 0-590-47365-4	**Plain City,** Virginia Hamilton	$5.99 US
☐ 0-590-45881-7	**From the Notebooks of Melanin Sun,** Jacqueline Woodson	$5.99 US
☐ 0-590-48142-8	**Toning the Sweep,** Angela Johnson	$5.99 US
☐ 0-590-42792-X	**My Brother Sam is Dead,** James Lincoln Collier and Christopher Collier	$5.99 US
☐ 0-590-46715-8	**When She Hollers,** Cynthia Voigt	$5.99 US
☐ 0-439-36850-2	**Winter,** John Marsden	$5.99 US

Available Wherever You Buy Books or Use This Order Form

Scholastic Inc., P.O. Box 7502, Jefferson City, MO 65102

Please send me the books I have checked above. I am enclosing $_____ (please add $2.00 to cover shipping and handling). Send check or money order—no cash or C.O.D.s please.

Name_____Birth date_____

Address_____

City_____State/Zip_____

Please allow four to six weeks for delivery. Offer good in U.S.A. only. Sorry, mail orders are not available to residents of Canada. Prices subject to change.

SCHOLASTIC and associated logos are trademarks and/or registered trademarks of Scholastic Inc.

◼ SCHOLASTIC

PNT0104